Screaming
and Other Tales

ENJOY!

And give me a review

on Amazon.com

Henry Neil

2/28/2023

Screaming

and Other Tales

by
Harry Neil

Donella Press
Kirksville, Missouri

Copyright © 2020 Harry Neil. All rights reserved.

No part of this work may be reproduced, distributed, or transmitted in any form or by any means, including photocopying, recording, or other electronic or mechanical methods, without the prior written permission from the publisher, except in the case of brief quotations embodied in critical review or other non-commercial uses permitted by copyright law.

Cover art: Edvard Munch, *The Scream*, 1893. Public domain, image from Wikimedia Commons.

Names: Neil, Harry, author.
Title: Screaming and other tales / by Harry Neil.
Description: First printing. | Kirksville, Missouri : Donella Press, [2020]
Identifiers: ISBN: 9781734260120 (paperback) | 9781734260137 (ebook) | LCCN: 2020922746
Subjects: LCSH: Time—Fiction. | Reality—Fiction. | Memory— Fiction. | Future, The—Fiction. | History—Fiction. | Space and time—Fiction. | Imaginary places—Fiction. | Mind and reality—Fiction. | Gender identity—Fiction. | LCGFT: Short stories. | Science fiction.
Classification: LCC: PS3614.E44284 S37 2020 | DDC: 813/.6-- dc23

Printed and bound in the United States of America.

First printing, December 2020.

Published by Donella Press, Kirksville, Missouri.
Visit donellapress.com

For
Leona and Elizabeth

They believed in me
and taught me
to believe in myself.

Contents

Foreword

In his lifetime, William Sidney Porter (1862–1910) churned out over six hundred short stories under the pen name of O. Henry. His trademark surprise endings to his mellow, humorous, and ironic tales made him for years America's favorite—possibly the country's still favorite—storyteller.

Similarly, North Carolinian Harry Neil, who discovered "freedom" (his word) by moving to the desert near Palm Springs after a computer programming career, has become popular among his readers with many similarly twisted endings to what he calls his "short pieces." And, as with O. Henry's eclectic themes, Neil's tales range broadly, from spookiness to futurism, from madness to fantasy.

Readers of these stories have hailed them as "fantastic and wildly imaginative," "heartwarming," "pure genius," "edgy and hallucinogenic," and "a joy to read." You will certainly be entertained and, perhaps even, as one reader before you said, "entranced."

David Wallace
Palm Springs, California
April 2020

David Wallace is a nationally published writer whose work has been reviewed by *The New York Times* as "inspired," and who was hailed by the late nationally syndicated columnist Liz Smith as "the maestro of entertainment history."

Ruby, You're Like a Song

This ain't a hearin' or anything formal like that, but we got two people dead, one of 'em a deputy, and I need to figger out why. I been chief in Tin City for over twenty years, and ain't nothin' like this ever happened before. Last real murder we had was that Rodney Miller thing back in '75, and that was, Lord, musta been fifteen years ago now. I just need to get my head around this thing and figger out what has to be done. You're the people saw it all, and I need you all to tell me just what it was you saw. May's bringin' in Louise Clark; apparently she saw some of it too."

Chief Jasper Tucker dumped some powdered creamer into his big coffee mug. He was a portly man, with thinning red hair and the beginnings of a double chin. His office was a melding of police station and man cave. The walls sported a buck head, a sailfish, and the weapons used to capture them. "I know it all started with Ruby, but I can't for the life of me figure how or why. Jarvis, you're the one shot her, right? Tell me just what happened."

Deputy Jarvis Wright shifted nervously from one foot to the other. "Well, she come runnin' down the road, like she was comin' from her house, you know. Only she was screamin' and wavin' her arms all around like a crazy woman. Well, I reckon she *was* a crazy woman, 'cause she headed right fer Billy Ray and she pulled out this gun and put a bullet right through his head. Real clean shot too. Don't know how she did it so clean, the state she was in. And with that funny old pistol too."

Jarvis raked a bony hand through jet black hair. "Then she just kept screamin' and cryin' and jumpin' up and down and wavin' that gun around. I figured she was gonna kill us all if nobody stopped her, so I shot her. Didn't aim to kill her, you understand, but I reckon I didn't have time to be careful, so I reckon I did. She went down kinda slow, and more sobbin' than screamin', kinda like she couldn't really catch her breath. I don't think she even knew she was shot. It was kinda like she just gave up and crumpled down on her own, only by the time she hit the ground she was dead."

Jarvis took a deep breath. "I ran up to her to try to do whatever I could, but there wasn't nothin'. I just stood there and looked for a minute. Never saw anything like it, you know? She was wearin' this funny dress, not like anything I ever saw on her before. And her face was all red and wet, and slobber all over her chin. She was actually foamin' at the mouth. It hit my mind that she mighta actually been bit by a mad dog, but I didn't stop to think about that. I ran over here fast as I could and called for the medics. Don't know why—nothin' they could do. She was dead."

Jarvis sat down heavily. "That's about it. Damnedest thing I ever saw. Damnedest thing I ever want to see. I ain't gonna sleep tonight; I know I ain't."

The chief looked puzzled. "What did you mean about a funny old pistol, Jarvis?"

Deputy Mike Gowan piped up. "It's just like that one Lee-Roy tried to use when you raided his liquor still, Chief, remember? A matched set of old duelin' pistols. You wouldn't think LeeRoy'd know anything about duelin' pistols or antique ammunition, but I guess to him guns were just guns. You kept the one, but apparently LeeRoy hid the other one somewhere, and I guess Ruby knew where to find it and how to use it. LeeRoy woulda taught her how to scare off strangers who got too close to the still. Anyway, we got both of them now—the guns, I mean. They're single-shot pistols, but course Jarvis didn't know that in time."

Mike puttered over to the coffee machine and started mixing a brew. "Now I don't know why anybody's surprised. Everybody knows Ruby's crazy. My pa calls her Delta Dawn, from that song, you know? 'All the folks 'round Brownsville say she's crazy.' This was bound to happen sometime, or somethin' like it. It's what we get for lettin' crazies run 'round on the streets. There oughta be laws."

"There's another song that's better," the chief said thoughtfully. "A lot older, though. 'They say, Ruby, you're like a song. You don't know right from wrong.' Used to be real popular, back before rock 'n' roll. That was around '52, '53. I remember 'cause of that new Studebaker Starliner. That was one beautiful car! Lord, how I wanted that car!" He stared into space, remembering. "I swore that when I was old enough to drive, I was gonna get me a Starliner, and I was gonna name her 'Ruby,' after that song. Course, by the time I was old enough, I had other interests. So I never did get one."

"Prob'ly just as well," Mike said. "My grandpa had one, and he said it was made outa tin foil; you could bend it like a garden hose. Couldn't even open the door if the thing was up on a jack. Pretty, but dumb, kinda like Addie." Mike and Jarvis exchanged knowing glances.

"Now don't you boys go trashin' Addie Thompson," the chief said. "She does the best she can. After all, look what she's got for parents."

The change of subject visibly relaxed Jarvis. "Ain't that one of them telescopin' arguments?" he asked. "I reckon Ike and Laura Thompson had parents too. How far back you suppose this goes?"

4 × Harry Neil

"Not Ike," Mike volunteered. "They said he was a virgin birth. Least his mama did. Personally, I got my doubts."

"Boys!" The chief pounded his desk. "Billy Ray's lyin' down in Sutton's Parlor with a bullet in his head! This ain't the time..."

───●●●───

Mercifully, the door opened, and May Watson brought in Louise Clark, a dark-haired scarecrow of a woman in a plain black dress. "Thank you for comin', Louise." The chief poured her a coffee. "You take it black, right? What did you see?"

Louise was more than willing to share. "Well Jasper, I get an hour for lunch, and I always take my sandwich over to the park. It was real nice out there today, so I musta stayed there for pretty much the whole hour, just watchin' the world go by, you know? Anyway, Ruby was there too, just sittin' on a bench across the park. First time I'd seen her for a while—no, wait—I saw her just yesterday. She was goin' into Foster's store just as I was goin' back to work, so you might wanna talk to Bertha. She runs the register at Foster's in the middle of the day."

Jasper motioned her to stop. He punched a button on his intercom. "May, call Ted Foster and tell him to send Bertha over here for a few minutes. We need her. He can run his own register for a little while." He turned back to Louise, and she went on.

"Do you know, Mr. Mitchell won't even let me have a cash register? That man is a piece of work! He sits up there in that barbed-wire cage where he can see the whole store, and he registers every sale himself. When I sell somethin' I hafta put the sales slip and the money on that chain thing and it rattles up to him. He makes the change and rattles it back to me. Ain't nobody used that kinda thing for twenty, thirty years. Nobody but Mr. Mitchell, I mean. When it breaks, he can't get parts for weeks. What a miser! I don't know why I put up with it!

"Anyway, today Ruby was just sittin' there. I didn't pay her no mind, except to wonder why she was all gussied up in that tacky blue taffeta dress. I never thought of Ruby and taffeta in the same breath before. She's more the feed-sack-frock kind, you know. I figured somethin' special musta been goin' on in that crazy head of hers, and she musta pulled out her old prom dress."

The chief interrupted her again. "Prom dress? What's a prom dress got to do with anything?"

Louise smiled indulgently. "I forget, Jasper. You're a man. What would you know? You see, most any girl's still got that dress she wore to her high-school prom hangin' way back in the back of the closet. Ain't no use no more—too fancy for church, or for anything else that's like' to happen in a little place like Tin City. But she keeps it 'cause it's the only thing reminds her o' what used to be.

"When she's happy, it reminds her o' bein' a pretty young girl with the boys linin' up to dance with her. When she's sad, it reminds her o' what mighta been, and how different things turned out from what they oughta. Sometimes when she's by herself she takes it out and holds it up to her in front o' the mirror. Most girls don't ever try to put it on—after all, she ain't that skinny no more—and maybe sometimes she thinks she oughta throw it away. But she don't, 'cause that'd be throwin' away her girlhood."

Louise got a faraway look in her eyes, remembering. "It's like in that Glenn Campbell song, Jasper, 'Dreams of the Everyday Housewife,' 'She touches the house dress that suddenly disappears. Just for the moment she's wearin' the gown that broke all their minds back so many years.' Lord, I loved that song. Made me think maybe there was one man out there somewhere understood. Anyway, if a girl's lucky enough to still be skinny and fit in that dress, she may put it on once or twice in her life, in some real special, private moment when she feels like a girl again, and when ain't nobody but her gonna see. Or maybe in some awful moment when she's so down she's actually gonna kill herself, and she wants them that finds her to remember her how she used to be."

"It's the truth, Boss," Mike interrupted. "My wife has one, and she treats it like some kind of religious relic."

Louise didn't appreciate the interruption, and she went on, "So when I saw Ruby all dressed up so funny, and when it flashed in my mind that maybe she was wearin' her prom dress, I figured something really important was happenin', at least in her mind. But since she's crazy, I figured whatever it was prob'ly just that, just in her mind. We've all got used to ignorin' Ruby since she's got so crazy, 'specially since Lee-Roy's gone.

"Anyway, there wasn't nothin' goin' on, really. Almost nobody about, you know. I saw Wilbur Paget pull up in that old red Travelall and put his boy Walter on the bus to Raleigh. He's takin' agerculture at State, you know. And I saw Carrie Anderson pushin' the Johnson baby aroun' in a stroller. She babysits, you know, while Becky's teachin' school. But that was about it.

Louise finished her coffee and covered the cup with her hand as both deputies jumped to refill it. She continued, "Then just as I was gettin' up to go, I saw Billy Ray pull up in the police pickup truck. Nothin' special about that, I reckon, but I saw Ruby jump up and stare at him. She looked like she'd been cryin', but then all of a sudden, she got real upset. She yelled out and she ran at Billy Ray like the Devil. She was yellin' and screamin' and carryin' on like a banshee. I never saw her like that. I never saw nobody like that. Billy Ray just kinda stared at her, and I don't know if he said anything or not, but then she turned around all of a sudden and headed back towards her house, runnin' like a scared rabbit. I figgered whatever it was had happened was over, and I was gonna be late gettin' back to my counter, so I went back to work. Mr. Mitchell don't put up with my bein' late. He's a penny-pinchin' miser, you know. And now I better get back there before he gets mad."

The chief nodded, "Thanks, Louise—that'll probably help us figger it out." Louise slipped out the door.

———◆•◆———

The chief packed his pipe thoughtfully. "So Walter Paget's already gone, huh? Sorry to hear that. Wanted to talk to him about some vandalism out on the highway. Somebody decorated up the old Christmas tree. Looked like one-a them toilet paper jobs you hear about frat boys doin'. I figger Walter's picked up some of them frat tricks from the boys at State, and maybe he's leadin' our local boys astray."

He took a few puffs, "I 'member one time him askin' why we don't decorate the old Christmas tree no more. I told him times had changed, and what with TV and all we couldn't get away with callin' it 'the world's biggest small-town Christmas tree' no more. And anyway, in the daytime anybody could tell it was just a big flagpole with lights strung down from the top to that old live oak tree at the bottom. It was a nice old tradition back then, but now's different. Anyway, somebody got the notion to decorate it up, and that's just vandalism. I told Billy Ray to go out there and clean it up, but I don't know if he ever got around to it, and now he's dead. Well, it's not important right now. We got bigger problems."

———◆•◆———

May brought in Bertha Miller. "I gotta be quick, Jasper. Mr. Foster made me clock out to come over here, so I'm not get-ting' paid for this." Bertha settled her little round body into a chair, her short legs dangling.

"We'll be quick," the chief assured her. "Just tell us when you saw Ruby last and what happened."

"Ruby?" Bertha studied the ceiling. "Well yeah, she was in the store just yesterday. Acted real funny. Pawed through all my dry goods like she was lookin' for somethin' special, but never said just what. Finally, she found a bolt o' taffeta she liked, and she bought the whole bolt. Cost her thirty-five dollars too. I remember I thought to myself, 'where's a wom-an like her get thirty-five dollars to spend on fancy stuff? And with LeeRoy gone and all.' But she had the money in her pocketbook, so she bought it, and off she went. Seemed happy as a lark, all of a sudden. Just danced outa there. I didn't think any more about it, cause everybody knows she's crazy, what with LeeRoy gone and all."

"You know," she reminded them, "she really misses that man. He just adored her, and he was always bringin' her flowers and candy and stuff. You wouldn't think it to look at him, but he was a real romantic, he was. He'd play her love songs on that old guitar, and sing to her like a teen-aged suitor. Sometimes he'd send her up to the attic to look out the dormer window, and he'd serenade her on her bal-cony with flamenco music. He could actually play that stuff just like a Spaniard. Sometimes he'd act out little romantic scenes with her—stuff from Broadway or Shakespeare—and she'd just lap it up, she would. 'Course she always played coy with him. Wouldn't let him get too sure of her, you know? She was a pretty wise woman back then, but not no more; now she's just lost. For all her coyness, she really loved that man. And she never got the chance to tell him.

"Reminds me of that Judy Garland song, remember? 'Ever since this world began, there is nothing sadder than a one-man woman, looking for the man that got away.'"

"Nothin' else happened?" the chief asked. "She didn't say nothin' out of the ordinary?"

"No Jasper, she didn't talk much, not even as much as usual. Kinda like she had a little secret she was keepin' to herself. No idea what it mighta been. A crazy woman probably has a lotta secrets she makes up and enjoys playin' 'round with. Can I get back to work?"

"Sure, Bertha. Thanks a lot for comin' over. Let me know if you think of anything else." As Bertha hurried out, the chief leaned back and stared at the ceiling. "Looks like maybe that wasn't a prom dress after all, boys. Looks like Ruby bought that taffeta just yesterday. Still don't make no sense though."

———•••———

May stuck her head in the door. "Chief, the mayor just called. Said they let LeeRoy out yesterday. Good behavior. Shouldn't somebody 'a' notified you about that?"

The chief bolted upright. "Hell, yes, somebody shouda! Another bureaucratic mess-up! Lord, this is the age of the snafu! Is he comin' this way?"

May came on into the room. "The mayor said he oughta been on the 12:30 bus. Anybody seen him?"

Just then Bertha burst back into the room. "Hey, you idiots!" she screamed. "What's that in that pickup out there? That's that yellow taffeta Ruby bought, ain't it? Somebody's shredded it to ribbons, they have! How'd it all get in that pickup? Well? Answer me, somebody! Somebody must know what's goin' on around here, don't they? Is this a police station or a loony ward?"

Everybody stared, first at Bertha, then at each other. Then they all spoke at once.

Jarvis: "*Yellow*? Good Lord! Boss, Ruby didn't buy *blue* taffeta for a *dress*, she bought *yellow* taffeta for *welcome ribbons*! That was a prom dress after all! And that wasn't *toilet paper* on that old oak tree, that was *yellow ribbons*!"

Mike: "Omigod! LeeRoy was playin' one of his romantic games! You know how that song goes, Boss. 'If I don't see a yellow ribbon round the old oak tree, I'll stay on the bus, forget about us, and put the blame on me!' Boss, Billy Ray destroyed Ruby's life just by cleanin' up that tree! We been singin' the wrong song!"

May was almost in tears. "Boss, you gotta get somebody to stop that bus, and get LeeRoy *off*! Boss, LeeRoy don't know what's happened here!"

The chief cradled his head for only a moment. "And he mustn't never, May. Ruby's dead, and LeeRoy never had nothin' in Tin City but Ruby. Even his liquor still was hid in somebody else's woods. Which would be worse, May, lettin' him go through life thinkin' Ruby didn't want him back, or knowin' she did want him, and it got her killed? Bringin' him back here now would just be cruel. Ruby's dead."

He tapped his pipe out in the ashtray. "Okay everybody, let's get back to work now. I know what happened, and I know who's gotta be called, and what papers gotta be filled out. And Jarvis, don't you worry. There'll be an investigation and all, but nothin's gonna happen to you. You didn't do nothin' wrong. Nobody's done nothin' wrong here. Like Mike said, we just been singin' the wrong song."

A Fondness for Murder

When a man finds that he is good at a thing, it is only natural that he should develop a fondness for it. That is probably why Boynton Fenwick developed a fondness for murder. It begs the question, though, of how he discovered that he was good at murder in the first place. For that, we can probably thank Millicent Kerr.

Not that Millicent was anxious to be murdered. To be sure, she had a reputation as a melancholy child, one given to taking long moody walks along the riverbanks, but one could not say that she was morbidly depressed; certainly not that she was suicidal. On the contrary, her schoolmistress would later say that Millicent was bright, competent, and even ambitious. "She dreamed of becoming the mistress of her own school for girls," Miss Clancy would say that fateful spring of '34, "and she actively pursued that goal in every aspect of her life."

Every aspect, that is, except for those long solitary walks. Only Millicent's one close friend and confidante, Maggie McAllister, knew the actual secret of those walks. Millicent had told Maggie that she walked alone to remember, to respect, and to commune with her lost mother. The mother who had cherished and nourished Millicent through her early childhood. The mother who had instructed Millicent that she must never let being a girl stand in the way of her dreams. The mother who had developed a quiet cough, then an aggressive cough. The mother who had gone away to Asheville to take the mountain air, and who had returned to Millicent in a mahogany coffin. The mother whom Millicent must never dishonor and never forget. The mother whose place in the home had been taken by a kind but inadequate stranger.

Millicent was as devoted to her father as to her mother, and his happiness was more important to her than her own. She understood that she must never allow any shrine to her mother's memory to intrude on the harmonious whole that her home had again become upon her father's remarriage, so she chose as her shrine the river. The river where she and her mother had walked and talked so often. The riverbanks where they had picnicked and shared their deepest secrets. Where they had thrown wildflowers into the lazy currents to watch them borne downstream, someday to merge their tattered remnants with the sea. Where they had talked of the soul and its inexplicable voyage into the infinite beyond. Millicent's riverside walks were spiritual exercises, sacraments that she could not share with any other living being.

Boynton Fenwick's eyes had always followed Millicent. Even as a child, long before he felt any stirrings in his loins, Boynton had understood that, while he knew no reason why he would pursue the fairer sex, that must inevitably change. It was a thing that happened to all boys, whether they wanted it or not, an unavoidable change in the plans for his life as he might see them now. Boynton assumed from an early age that, when the time came, Millicent Kerr would be the object of his attentions.

Perhaps that all began at that Fourth of July celebration in '26, when all the Rockport families gathered at the old bandshell to picnic, to sing, to give or hear speeches, and in general to socialize. The bandshell stood in a verdant park, with gently rolling knolls covered with green grass and punctuated with flowering shrubs that seemed always in bloom. The knolls formed terraces just made for the spreading of picnic blankets, so that all the picnickers would have a good view of the bandshell.

It happened, in '26, that the Fenwicks and the Kerrs chose adjacent spots to spread their picnic blankets. Boynton's father was the town optometrist, respectable but not pretentious, so Boynton, a scrawny little redhead in faded shorts, was allowed to run barefoot about the park. The Reverend Kerr, on the other hand, reigned over the prestigious Covenant Presbyterian Church, as well as a couple of rural congregations unable to afford their own pastors. The Kerrs were prim, proper, and oh, so respectable, so Millicent, arrayed in a stylish drop-waisted frock and patent-leather slippers, sat gravely on the family blanket and watched the proceedings with folded hands.

Everybody sang along as the band struck up a series of patriotic songs. Singing together is a great social lubricant, and as people began to mingle more freely, the band switched to popular songs of the day. It was as they sang Al Jolson's hit "I'm Sitting on Top of the World" that Boynton, munching his Cracker Jack and nursing his Nehi Orange, was struck by the little girl at his side. She was polished, poised, and pretty. He was rough, clumsy, and socially inept. Nevertheless, at that moment, Boynton set himself a new goal: he would watch over this delicate creature, and when the time came, she would be his.

———•••———

Narcissism is an original sin of the male of our species, and it masks from its sufferer the fact that others may well have their own plans for their lives. We can probably blame that condition for Boynton's failure to mention his plans for future affections to the intended object of those affections. It is doubtful whether Millicent shared Boynton's interest, or even noticed it, but that mattered little to him. In those days of innocence, Boynton's eyes followed Millicent much as an investor's eyes follow the daily market reports.

That all changed one bright May afternoon, as Miss Conklin was preparing to dismiss her class for the last time before the summer vacation. She congratulated all her brood for having passed their final exams and having earned the right to advance to the next grade in the fall. She heaped special praise upon Millicent Kerr. "Because of her hard work and studious habits," Miss Conklin said, "Millicent has earned a very special right. Millicent will skip the fifth grade!"

Boynton's blood ran suddenly cold. His intended had turned on him. Boynton was bright, precocious even, and he knew that he was as nimble with his times tables as Millicent could ever be. He could split a sentence into a subject and predicate with unerring accuracy. He could spell, even the stupid words like "bureau," and he knew that it was in 1492 that Columbus sailed the ocean blue. What had Millicent done that he had not? Why was she forsaking him? In Garrison Grammar School, each teacher ruled over a closed society, a walled kingdom within which its subjects found all their friends and made all their social contacts. Once Millicent and Boynton did not share a grade, she would be as inaccessible to him as that shiny Western Flyer bicycle that his father would not buy from the Western Auto store.

———•◦•———

Boynton's father, Needham Fenwick, did not believe in bicycles. Back in the nineties, he had broken his arm trying to learn to ride one. The arm had mended crooked, and the doctors had broken it again so that it would grow back straight. To Needham Fenwick, the bicycle was a demonic contraption. No child of Needham Fenwick's would ever ride a bicycle.

Nothing burns the heart as do intentions thwarted, so while Boynton's eyes still followed Millicent when possible, it was now with enmity, even hatred. Now hatred, especially secret hatred, is a cancerous thing. It starts as a single cell and grows to dominate its host. The once carefree Boynton Fenwick evolved into a bitter, scheming youth. With puberty, he grew from a scrawny kid into an Ichabod Crane of a teen, tall, sallow, and uncoordinated. His youthful beard grew in patchy and of an indeterminate color. He began to avoid his contemporaries, especially when they gathered to play sandlot baseball or to shoot hoops in the increasingly popular game of basketball. And when the fires of desire did kindle in Boynton's loins, he directed them not into amorous pursuit, but into revenge.

———•••———

So it was that when Millicent walked on the riverbank on a particularly blustery day in March, Boynton watched from the concealment of a myrtle copse, his fevered mind seething. How could he bring this false goddess down from her pedestal into the mire where she belonged? Fate intervened in the form of a sudden gust that snatched Millicent's yellow straw hat and sent it whirling in playful spirals. Boynton's pulse raced. The goddess had been uncrowned! He fixed his attention on the spiraling hat and with every nerve in his body, he pushed it down, down, onto the water. As if obeying his command, it dropped softly to the surface and settled there, and like a toy boat, it moored itself among the branches of a poplar tree that had toppled from the bank into the lazy stream. Boynton's body stiffened, his eyes glazed, and a terrible roar in his head resolved itself into a loud, endless loop of "I'm Sitting on Top of the World."

It all happened so fast, and so easily! Later, Boynton would not quite remember just how it did happen. How could it be that everything arranged itself so perfectly for him? The sudden wind, the fallen poplar, the easy path that tempted Millicent to navigate the fallen trunk to retrieve her property. More unbelievably, the big stick he found in his hand, the forked branch just made for grasping a slender neck and holding it under water, and then for tucking it under a submerged limb to be found later by others.

Nobody ever suspected any foul play. It was obvious that Millicent had tried to retrieve her hat, had slipped, had thrashed in the water, had been foiled by her petticoats, and had been caught by an underwater branch. The family mourned. The village mourned. Even Boynton pretended to mourn, but inside he was ecstatic. He had pulled it off. He had vanquished the evil one.

———•••———

When circumstances align themselves for a man, when he falls victim to an incredible sequence of coincidences that work to his benefit, it is natural for him to believe that he has skill. Many a fortune has been won through just such accidental circumstances, and many such fortune has then been lost through just such false beliefs. Man is a creature of great ego, and he is not easily swayed by mere facts. Occasionally, very occasionally indeed, the final coincidence is that the incident has in fact exposed genuine talent.

So it was with Boynton Fenwick. After pondering the circumstances of the demise of Millicent Kerr, Boynton came to believe that he had carried off a difficult task, an especially difficult task for a sixteen-year-old, with special ease. He pondered this fact for some weeks, until he came to realize that the important aspect of Millicent's demise was no longer that it was Millicent, but that it was a demise. Examining his soul from a fresh perspective, Boynton recognized a hitherto unknown gnawing hunger. Like a youth who has stolen his first real kiss, Boynton mused, "I really want to do that again."

———•••———

Opportunity does not knock as it did with Millicent every day, so Boynton's ambition seethed within him for a long period of watchful waiting. When opportunity did next present itself, it leaped upon him with the suddenness and intensity of an earthquake. Boynton was walking along Elm Street, going it doesn't matter where, and lost in thoughts that no longer matter, when little Billy Barnhouse suddenly swerved into his path on a shiny green Murray Streamline Velocipede. Boynton froze. Images of that unattainable Western Flyer exploded into his mind's eye, pushing all rational thought aside. This child, this worthless slip of a child, this mere worm upon the face of the earth, had been gifted with one of the finest vehicles that money could buy, at least for his age group. Boynton, on the other hand, Boynton, about whom the sun and moon, about whom the entire universe turned, was denied even a common bicycle.

There was no justice! But there could be revenge! And the strains of "I'm Sitting on Top of the World" began to play in Boynton's head.

Again, opportunity was quickly followed by means, and again, Boynton would not later recall the exact details. There was no river on Elm Street, but there was, at this particular moment, the Widow Morrison's old maroon LaSalle sedan, lumbering along towards the A&P down at the corner of

Second Street. The good widow was neither keen to observe nor quick to respond, her attention being focused on keeping the LaSalle's hood ornament, a miniature cavalier, aligned with the curb. The late Doc Morrison, believing women to be simple creatures incapable of complex thought, had taught his wife to drive an automobile using the most fundamental of techniques. "Keep the little man walking on the curb," he'd instructed her.

The widow was unprepared for the unexpected, so the green three-wheeler was beneath her whitewalled tires before she could react. When the housewives of Elm Street responded to her frantic horn blasts, they did not think to scan the street for any other persons. May Hudson, being watchful of the rising time of her special pumpernickel loaves, did note that it was exactly ten minutes to four in the afternoon when the cacophony arose.

Again, nobody suspected foul play. It was obvious that little Billy, absorbed in the delight of his new toy, simply pedaled into the path of the LaSalle, and that there was nothing Widow Morrison could have done to avoid the accident. Leticia Barnhouse was chided for not having watched the child more closely, but chided very lightly indeed, she being the grieving mother. The widow was not chided at all, but local citizens did note that the next time the LaSalle sallied forth, it was not Widow Morrison at the wheel, but Lucius Baldwin.

———•••———

Lucius could neither read nor write, but his driving was legend. Everyone in Rockford, probably everyone in all of Rockfish County, believed Lucius had been driving the big black Lincoln Police Flyer that had led Sheriff Colin Ferguson to his death in '24. The Lincoln was surely ferrying Rockfish

County moonshine to the lucrative military speakeasies of Norfolk and Newport News. Its big V8 engine easily outpaced the sheriff's Essex, but Ferguson persisted in his pursuit and the Essex wound up upside down and burning in Rockfish Creek.

No one ever saw that Lincoln in Rockfish County again, but a shiny yellow Stutz Bearcat took up residence beside the tarpaper shack that Lucius shared with his ancient grandmother Dorcas. Dorcas was born a slave, and she remembered Reconstruction all too well. Perhaps that's why it was her policy never to cause trouble of any kind, and perhaps *that's* why it was Lucius's policy to cause as much trouble as possible. Prohibition and youth offered Lucius fertile ground to cultivate that policy. That, and the appearance of the Stutz, was evidence enough to convict him in the public mind.

Repeal, maturity, and a hunting accident quickly mellowed Lucius's habits and reputation, and by the time of the velocipede incident, the Morrison clan—the widow had been prolific in her productive years—considered him an appropriate, even an excellent choice for their mother's chauffeur.

———◆••◆———

Reflecting back on the velocipede incident, Boynton marveled again at how easily things had organized themselves in his favor. No one would ever have reason to suspect foul play, but should they, no one would ever have reason to put Boynton at the scene. Even if, in some incomprehensible way, someone did think to question him, he had an ironclad alibi. Maggie Harrison would surely testify that at exactly ten minutes to four on that day, Boynton engaged her in a heated debate about her rigid enforcement of the sign hanging over her lunch counter saying, "baked potato only after 4PM." Nobody would ever think to question Maggie's word, she being a fairly simple sort, and Maggie herself would never think of how easily a lone customer could reset the lunch-counter clock while she bent to the task of tending her baking potatoes.

It was all too perfect. Not only had Boynton been the benefactor of another incredible sequence of coincidences, but apparently, he had talent, and talent must not be hidden under a bushel. Talent must be displayed, if only in private and to oneself. Talent must be exercised.

———•••———

When a man has found his destiny, when he has suddenly stopped spinning like a weathercock and pointed himself resolutely in one direction, he may find hitherto unsuspected powers of concentration. He may suddenly abandon cherished avocations and replace sleep with restless scheming.

So it was with Boynton Fenwick. He was acutely aware that his last victim, a mere child, was beneath his station, and that his fine talents should not be wasted upon the inconsequential. It was time to select a target worthy of his newfound skills, one whose demise would be noticed and appreciated far and wide. It was time for a carefully planned test case that would establish, in his own mind if not publicly, just what Boynton Fenwick, this new Boynton Fenwick, this master of crime, was capable of doing. Abandoning his extensive stamp collection, Boynton brooded and schemed, schemed and brooded, and gradually formulated a plan.

———•••———

Miss Ruth Conklin, the hated Miss Conklin, the very Miss Conklin who had foolishly promoted Millicent Kerr ahead of Boynton Fenwick, had made something of herself. What her life lacked in romance it compensated for in industry. She had become the first female principal of Garrison Grammar School, and then of Rockfish County Central High. Finally, she had advanced to become Superintendent of Schools for Rockfish County. This despite her female status and a determined letter campaign to the *Rockfish County Chronicle*, protesting that her well-documented heart condition rendered her unfit. Doc Mebane's public assurance that the lady's condition was well controlled by a simple regimen of digitalis must have dispelled most doubts at the time.

Nevertheless, those prior events laid a foundation for Boynton's new project. The hated Miss Conklin was now a public figure of some importance and visibility in the county, even beyond. Her achievements as a woman were widely admired, and occasionally she accepted invitations to speak before various important bodies. She would do nicely. Boynton planned and prepared, prepared and planned, and finally the appointed day arrived.

Incredibly, no one was suspicious when Superintendent Ruth Conklin suffered a fatal heart attack, falling from the podium while delivering an inspirational talk to an assembly of school superintendents from across the state. People were certainly distressed, upset, even frantic, but no one was suspicious. Letters to the *Chronicle* of the "I told you so" sort only reinforced the general idea that this was something that was inevitable and so needed no further explanation. It was obvious what had happened. No one even thought to wonder whether someone might have tampered with the departed's medical supplies, and no one would ever have thought to watch the cemetery in the wee hours, where a definitely inebriated Boynton Fenwick danced gleefully upon the fresh-made grave, the strains of "I'm Sitting on Top of the World" roaring in his head.

————•••————

From that day, Boynton became a dedicated schemer. He had a new avocation, one that required a certain cunning and a good bit of planning. He realized that he needed the trust of the community at large. He must be a person above suspicion. He must have power in Rockfish County. He must have friends, important friends, very important friends. He set about to gain them.

In every small city there is a cadre of Men Who Matter, men who, because of wealth, office, or force of personality, cause the wheels of the city to turn. These men form bonds, and they gather to drink whiskey, hunt deer, and play poker. Boynton was, naturally, never a member of this group. Not only was he far too young to matter, but he preferred sherry to whiskey, he abhorred hunting, and he found poker crude and pointless. Nevertheless, he realized that, if he were to pursue his new avocation, he must cultivate these men, even somehow have power over them.

In every small city there is also a cadre of Women Who Matter, formed largely of the wives of the Men Who Matter, and distinguished by their power to exclude any woman not deemed worthy from their society. These women gather to drink tea, breed roses, and play pinochle. Boynton instinctively cultivated these women. He learned the arcane skills associated with the tea service. He planted a rose garden and made certain that at least one plant from the garden of every important woman grew there. He developed skill at pinochle, including the skill of not winning when winning would be impolitic. In short, he learned to fawn, and in so doing, he developed an invisible power of his own. Boynton's scrawny appearance and bumbling awkwardness set him apart from other men. Ladies rightly recognized in Boynton a soul unstained by carnal lust, which clearly separated him from the throng of menfolk who, according to the age-old "battle of the sexes," were regarded as the enemy. That made it natural for them to accept Boynton as one of their own number.

They failed, though, to discern within Boynton a soul heavily stained with a much more lethal lust, and when Boynton admired Stella Kelly's football mums, to her delight, she completely failed to see his private vision of those mums as a spray on her casket.

Among the Women Who Matter of Rockford, Boynton was known as "that *nice* Boynton Fenwick." Being a favorite of the Rockford ladies gave Boynton implicit influence over Rockford's influential men, and that came in handy several times. Perhaps most important, when Pearl Harbor was attacked in '41, and when most able-bodied young American men went to war, either voluntarily or through the draft, Boynton stayed at home in Rockford. Even though he was scrawny, uncoordinated, and weak, he was still eminently draftable. But for reasons never questioned and never made public, Boynton's name simply never came up before his draft board.

———◦•◦———

Boynton spent his free time deep in thought, inventing clever and unusual ways to dispatch his fellows, and he found ways to implement many of these inventions over his fourteen-year career in Rockfish County. Many of these murders were quite trivial, but some were most complex. The one targeting Judge Henry Carter, for instance, required Boynton to travel to Mexico to procure certain controlled substances. That trip rates special mention for another reason. It was while Boynton was in Mexico, supposedly to celebrate his twenty-first birthday, that Needham and Laura Fenwick died in their sleep, victims of a faulty floor furnace.

Needham Fenwick had dreamed all his life of spending a leisurely retirement traveling the world, and he had planned accordingly. He and Laura had lived frugally, saved aggressively, and invested wisely. Clarence Townsend, the executor of Needham's will, found a surprisingly robust portfolio. Agreeing with Needham's contention that his son lacked any concept of managing money or running a business, Clarence followed Needham's instructions to safely provide for Boynton. He sold Needham's optometry practice, added those funds to the portfolio, and arranged a steady monthly income for Boynton.

On his return, Boynton made a very public display of mourning. Then he bought a bicycle—and not a simple Western Flyer, but a fully equipped Schwinn Autocycle Deluxe. This even though he had just inherited his father's '38 Hudson Terraplane. He also bought a phonograph and several covers of "I'm Sitting on Top of the World."

Boynton was now his own man, and able to spend his time as he wished. When he was not inventing new crimes, he played those phonograph records and browsed his collection of certain back issues of the *Chronicle*, those detailing his past crimes, or at least the publicly visible aspects of those crimes. Most were reported as "accidents" or "unexplained events." Boynton delighted in the fact that not one soul who read the *Chronicle* had ever noticed that something must be dreadfully wrong in Rockfish County. Compared to his own advanced state the local police seemed gullible or outright incompetent. He never considered that an incredible sequence of coincidences, indeed an incredible sequence of such sequences, might have worked to protect him from detection for all those years. Boynton much preferred the simpler explanation—he was *good* at murder, and not just good at doing it, but good at getting away with it.

———•••———

When a man loves his work, and when that work has the prospect of going on without end, a man's enthusiasm is bound to grow, perhaps to the point of giddiness. Boynton Fenwick became so engrossed in his murderous avocation that he thought of nothing else. It was fortunate that he had inherited a house and a modest income, and so had no need of employment; else body and soul might not have clung together. Of course, his projects did incur some expenses— witness that trip to Mexico—so Boynton lived simply and frugally, directing his resources where the most pleasure would result.

With the giddiness of success may come carelessness, and with carelessness, danger. The day came when Boynton made his first real mistake. After arranging for an alcoholic itinerant laborer named Leroy leFey to be struck and killed by a speeding midnight freight train, Boynton exercised his usual rite of joyfully but cautiously collecting and removing any evidence before the crime was discovered. On this occasion, joy dominated caution, and he foolishly left the dead man's legs lashed together. Later, noting that that rope was missing, he realized with some horror that the authorities would know that the victim had not simply wandered, in an alcoholic haze, into the path of the freighter. This time they would call it murder.

True, nothing could link Boynton with the murder, but Rockford was not a big city, and there were only so many local people to suspect. Of course the railroad brought vagrants in and out and through town all the time, but if the perpetrator came that way he was surely long gone and almost untraceable. So Rockfish County Sheriff Lloyd Arthur would probably not waste too many resources investigating that angle. Boynton was bright, brilliant even, but also a bit paranoid, and long before any figure of authority could question him, he imagined those eyes watching his every move. It was time, he decided, to put his special skills on exhibit for the world to see. It was time to take the actions calculated so carefully over recent years. At the age of twenty-nine, Boynton thought it was time for his *magnum opus*.

Boynton visited the newly reopened Rockford Studebaker franchise—"*First by far with a postwar car*"— and bought a scarlet 1947 "which way is it going" Starlight Coupe. Rudolph Whitehead, anxious to return his Studebaker dealership to its prewar prosperity, was more than willing to arrange credit, but Boynton elected to pay cash. Rudolph did not find that strange, as Boynton's modest lifestyle had earned him the reputation of a saver.

The Rockford Ladies' Pinochle Club met Thursdays for lunch and play, with hostess responsibilities rotating among the members. That Thursday, the ladies were meeting at the home of the widowed Leticia Barnhouse of Elm Street. As Boynton approached the neo-Victorian decked in green and orange shingles, Marla Highsmith happened to glance out the window, and she chortled, "Letty, that *nice* Boynton Fenwick is coming up your walk." Mrs. Barnhouse beamed as she ushered Boynton into her parlor, crowded with loveseats, armchairs, and service tables, and offered him a seat in soft pink-flowered armchair. Boynton admired new frocks and hairdos, accepted tea and a cookie, and engaged in some fawning flattery before he finally announced the reason for his visit. He had typed out his Last Will and Testament, and he needed witnesses to his signature. Would any two of the ladies do him that favor?

Any lady would welcome the opportunity to perform a service so simple, yet so important, for that *nice* Mr. Fenwick, especially in the presence of her peers, so the competition was keen. Boynton finally selected Leticia Barnhouse and Harriet Arthur, the sheriff's wife, for the honor, and he appeased the others with the promise that as time passed and situations changed, there would surely be codicils to be signed and witnessed. After the selected ladies had signed, he rose from his chair, bowed slightly, then donned his fedora and said his goodbyes, going forth to meet his destiny with a chorus of "I'm Sitting on Top of the World" ringing in his head.

———•••———

The 1:27 express did not stop in Rockford. It picked up and deposited mail using the traditional hook and kick technologies, which only required that it slow down a bit. As its whistle sounded the warning for the several Rockford crossings, it was travelling about seventy miles per hour. The streets were deserted—the midday August sun kept most people indoors—so the train could have passed through unnoticed, but that was not to be.

There were few witnesses, but that mattered little, as there was never any question as to what had happened. Scarlet bits of Studebaker and of Boynton Fenwick still clung to the cowcatcher when the engineer finally brought the train to a stop almost a mile beyond the crossing.

The sheriff's officers found the will Boynton had left prominently displayed on his writing desk. It was signed and witnessed and ever so proper, but the contents were shocking. The authorities deemed it necessary to bypass policy and make the will public, and the *Chronicle* printed it in its entirety the very next day. Rockfish County was scandalized. Letters poured into the *Chronicle's* offices. For a time, the two lady witnesses feared to show their faces anywhere in the county. Sheriff Arthur had no real defense against accusations of gross negligence, and reluctantly submitted his resignation. Within two weeks, the retired sheriff and his witness wife filed for divorce, citing "irreconcilable differences."

Boynton's will instructed that a court-appointed executor should liquidate his property and portfolio. He listed thirty-seven names and dates, beginning with Millicent Kerr in '34 and ending with LeRoy LeFey in '47, each with details of the true manner of death and a proud claim of Boynton's role in those events. The will instructed that the executor divide the estate equally among the survivors of these thirty-seven murder victims "in recognition of the great personal joy that these persons afforded me during my life." Since Boynton had no other family, he had omitted Needham and Laura Fenwick from the list.

Several of the families refused this bequest outright, but most considered it no more than their due—and a small compensation indeed for their loss. The *Chronicle* and its letter writers debated for some time whether Boynton's will was about remorse or about braggadocio. Few recognized the truth: that it was just the simple gratitude of a complex man who had unfortunate skills and a fondness for murder.

Miss Julia

Nobody even noticed Julia when she shuffled into the shabby little hospice. The lobby was drab and unwelcoming, and not even the holiday music playing on the tinny little radio could cheer the room's gray hopelessness. Julia took off her shawl and overcoat as she passed the aide on duty, who didn't even look up from her charting. No problem; Julia knew her way. Frank Murphy, bed 6-A, down the left hallway.

The room was squalid and smelled of urine and disease. He was lying deathly still until she gently touched his face. He opened his eyes and they filled with tears. "You came," he whispered.

"Yes," she replied softly. "You rest."

She moved to the head of the rickety bed and took up *the position*, cradling his head in her hands, one on each temple, and it came. First a trickle, then a stream, and then a raging torrent of images, sounds, sensations, all the stuff of a life lived long and now dying. Occasionally one image would thrust itself into the foreground and hang there for just an instant before being swept away by the flood. Some she recognized: Elvis, Kennedy, the Space Shuttle. Some were related: a red-haired girl, later a pretty young woman, then a happy bride, then a face contorted in despair, and finally frozen in death. Some were just emotions—great joy, abject terror, wrenching guilt.

Eventually Julia's strength began to fade, but mercifully, the stream grew pale and indistinct, then gray, and finally black. Still she stood there, too exhausted to move.

When they found her there, still clutching the dead man's temples, they assumed that she was a grieving relative. They brought a chair and seated her while they did the necessary tasks. Later, the orderly who had pried her hands away would recall that they were cold, and that an icy sensation crept up his own arms to the elbows.

Nobody noticed when Julia finally arose and slipped out into the night with her coat and scarf. As she reached the curb, a city bus pulled up and opened its door for her. "Miss Julia," the driver nodded recognition. She got in and took the seat nearest the door when the young man sitting there rose and offered it. He was the only other passenger on the bus. Julia offered no fare, and none was asked.

After driving for some time in silence, the driver pointed to a small brightly lit diner on the other side of the street. "Paddy's Place makes the best Irish stew in town, Miss Julia. Maybe you should try it." She rose silently and got off. She made her way across the street, the few late holiday shoppers paying no mind to a nondescript old woman bundled up against the cold.

The diner was not familiar to her. "Miss Julia," the counter waitress acknowledged, "I'll get your tea." Moments later she was back with a steaming teapot and hot bread and butter. A bowl of hearty beef stew followed. Julia ate slowly and deliberately, sopping the last of the gravy with her bread. "I'll bring more," the waitress volunteered. Julia offered no payment, and none was asked.

As she took her threadbare coat from the rack by the door, the night manager took another and held it for her. "Take this one, Miss Julia," he said. "It's cold out there, and this one is warmer."

There were benches in a small park across a side street, so she sat there in the darkness and collected her thoughts.

A sign said "Park Closes at Sundown," but the beat cop who passed her did not make an issue. He only doffed his cap. "Miss Julia."

The noise of the city seemed somehow distant and non-intrusive, and the old questions flooded her mind. Who were these desperate outcasts who summoned her in their final hour of need? How did they make contact, and how did they even know of her? Why was she already known to anybody who could help her, but a complete stranger to everyone else?

And who was she? Had she ever been young? Did she have family of her own? Had anyone ever called her their wife or mother? Was someone somewhere even now waiting for her return? They were the same questions that haunted her any time she took the time to rest.

But as always, they would have to wait, for already her next task was becoming clear. One street north and four blocks to the left, at 2740 Harrison, there was a seedy hotel. One flight up, room 225 would be unlocked. His name was Alfred, and he needed her.

Now.

Screaming

"Your hands are screaming," Moira explains, watching my compulsively wringing hands. "You've seen things, maybe even done things, that you can't afford to remember. Your conscious mind won't remember, and your mouth won't scream. But when you move too close to those forbidden memories, your subconscious mind remembers, and it's able to get to your hands, and they scream."

Moira is my friend. Moira is probably my only friend—at least my only real friend. Oh, everybody is kind. People know they need to be kind to anybody who's come back from over there only half a man. People in London have suffered enough, from those screaming rockets and bombs, to know that it's been a terrible war, and that the men who've sacrificed their very sanity to it deserve their kindness. So kind people open doors for me and offer me their chairs. But kindness is not friendship, and only Moira has given me real friendship.

I was born—reborn, actually—in hospital in London. As the world came into focus for me, it was her face that I saw. That simple, homely face, that comforting face, the kind of face that a dying man would beg to see as his world turned grey. That beautiful, angelic face, a face that a man reborn would imprint on.

As the world clarified, that face became a voice, and that voice became a comfort. Eventually, I found my own voice, and I learned to ask questions. I found out that there'd been a war, and that somehow, I was part of it. "When they found you over there," Moira explained, "you were burned, torn up, bloody, and too shell-shocked to even look for food or water. You were catatonic, except for your hands. You were constantly wringing your hands and clenching your fists, or rather they were doing it by themselves, and they still are. There was no way to know who you were or where you came from, but it was pretty obvious that under all that blood and grime was an Englishman in trouble, so they bundled you off across the channel for somebody else to deal with. The troops on the Continent had enough on their hands."

Apparently, I wound up in hospital in London, where Moira was nurse to about a hundred mangled men. She understood that she was the force that had to make them whole again, and she threw herself into that task with everything she had to give. She was my angel, she was my savior, and she became my friend. She made me human again.

Once I was awake and able to reason, I was shocked to realize that I remembered nothing at all. Alarmed, I became obsessed with remembering. Who am I? Where do I come from? Do I have family or loved ones who are looking for me? My only clues were my blonde hair and blue eyes and my London accent. I don't feel like a religious man, but in those days, I prayed God for a miracle.

They discharged me as soon as they could, because they needed that hospital bed for the really wounded. I had no money and no place to go—a man with no past has a hard time imagining any future—but Moira fixed that. There was nothing romantic in my relationship with Moira, but it still surprised me to learn that she had a husband named Ian. She brought him to hospital and let him explain. "You'll come with us," he said. "I lost me Mum last year, and now her old room is just being wasted." So, Moira and Ian took me home with them. I've got a bed and a window and an old writing desk full of paper and pens, old photographs, and other old-lady stuff.

Now I earn my keep as a sort of housekeeper for Moira and Ian. Somehow, I seem to know what to do to keep things shipshape, and I've discovered that I'm a fair cook. "You set a pretty good table," Ian says, being kind.

Being out of hospital isn't the same as being well. I have a couple of peculiar compulsions, like I'm always checking inside the saltcellar. "Checking for worms," I explain to Ian, improvising.

"It's okay," he always says, "Worms don't live in salt." Moira touches his hand, saying silently, "Be kind."

My dreams are just naked terror. I have a recurring nightmare of blackbirds flocking in the snow. When I reach for them, they rise shrieking and turn into screaming and striking dragons. The dragons' fiery breath strikes at my hands, and my hands writhe in agony. "Your hands are screaming," Moira says. "Someday you'll really remember, and you'll be able to really scream. Then it'll all be over, and your hands can rest."

Between chores, I spend long hours sitting at that old writing desk. I don't know why, but it just seems a safe wall between me and the world. But maybe it's a wall between me and my lost past. Or maybe a clue; was I a writer? I have pens and paper, but I have nothing to write. So I sit there.

———•••———

When I can, I wander about London, watching the people and the city pulling their lives back together now that the bombing is over. I search the streets and alleys, museums and pubs and lecture halls, any place where there's anything happening that might ring that deep, lost bell, any place I might find my miracle.

Today, Moira has a few odd hours, and she's walking with me. "I see too much dying at hospital," she explains. "Seems like I lose one of my blokes almost every week. It helps to walk through London and see the city coming back to life. It reminds me that this is a victory, after all, even with all the dying that still goes on. Ian's working overtime, so I finally have some time alone to just relax."

A sign on the door of a little hall says something about "Lessons from the War." Moira is not interested, but I am always looking for my miracle, and this could help. I win out, and the two of us go in. The program has already started, and the several dozen people there are all seated in circles around a little dais. We sit in the back, and I try to somehow hide my nervous hands. Nobody notices, though, because somebody is just finishing up talking about how nations must always be ready to take in refugees, and now all the people are applauding him politely.

The next speaker introduces himself as Paul somebody. At his signal, two stagehands wheel a small piano out through the audience and onto the dais. "We may never know everything that went on in those camps," Paul says, "but I narrowly escaped being in one myself, so I'm making it my goal to learn everything I can. We can piece together some of it from the things those people left behind. I've been mining the newspapers for articles on the camps, and I've been interviewing soldiers who saw them firsthand. I've heard about a child's rag doll soaked in blood and about a diary with lists of names with their death dates. And someone found this," he holds up several sheets of paper. "This is a copy of something that was originally jotted down on scraps of faded yellow paper. This is music of a sort. It's hastily scribbled, and it's not what you're probably used to calling music, but it may well be what that horror turned music into. See what you think."

Paul sits at the piano and strikes several loud discords. He pauses and begins to play a bizarre sequence of chords and notes. Some are loud, some soft, but most are discordant. Some flow together and some do not. There are sequences of notes that build up madness and intensity until finally bursting into a powerful discordant climax, like those crazy dreams that wake you with that "exploding head" phenomenon. There is nothing of Beethoven here, or even Shostakovich. If there is melody, it is not apparent. If there is meter, it is rough. If there is chord progression, it breaks the rules. But there is something else, some other kind of coherence, something more important than melody, more important than harmony, something that resonates in my mind, something that excites me, focuses me, possesses me completely. This music does not sing; it screams! This is the music of horror, and I know horror. Paul is not playing it right, because Paul was not there. I WAS THERE!

———•••———

I am weightless. I am floating. My body is beyond my control. It is drifting like a cloud down the aisle. It is floating onto the little dais. Paul sees me and freezes, hands shaped for the next chord, but frozen mid-air. Paul is afraid of me. Paul is terrified of my scarred face and my clawing hands. He jumps to his feet, face blanched. One stagehand grabs for me, but the other grabs for him, because that man and I know the same truth: *I do not know what is happening here, but I do know that IT MUST HAPPEN.* I move on.

Now I am sitting at that piano—or is it a writing desk—or is it a wall between me and the world? I see the keys, and they are blackbirds in the snow. Now my hands are reaching for those keys, reaching fearfully for those birds. My hands are moving by themselves; they're touching the keys, striking the keys. My hands pound the keys, and from the keys rise screaming dragons, and the dragons' fiery breath strikes and directs my hands and my hands obey! My hands have found their voice in that keyboard, and they are screaming, screaming! They scream the very music from Paul's papers, and I am not looking at the papers.

My hands pound out horrors that I do not remember: the horror of imprisonment, of torture, of pain; the horror of death, of death all around and death crouched under every shadow, of death poised to pounce upon the unwary, to pounce upon even the most wary. My hands scream of madness; of inhumanity and madness. They play the very notes and the very real meaning of the music of the copied sheets. I do not remember ever seeing that music, but the dragons know the music. The dragons do know the screaming music! The dragons *remember*! I *surrender everything* to the dragons. The dragons *command*, and my hands *obey*!

Now, the dragons command a change in the screaming music. It is no longer the music of the yellowed scraps, but it *is* the music of the dragons. My hands pound out horrors that I do not remember: the horror of tangles of barbed wire; of the pain as it tears through my flesh; of my terror as my blood spurts through the coils. My hands scream of panic, and of running; of running hard; of running so hard that I forget the pain. They scream the horror of darkness; of the black, impenetrable forest; of my fury, tearing my way through invisible underbrush; of breaking a path through impenetrable masses of brambles; of feeling those brambles tear my skin until I am covered with my own blood.

My hands scream the distant barking of dogs; the horror of realizing that they are following my blood trail, the terror of knowing that I cannot cover that trail, the desperation of hearing the dogs closing in, of knowing that the black forest holds no sanctuary for me. My hands scream the shock of feeling my humanity drain away, of becoming an animal, a wild beast with no conscience and no memory, and no thought but one, *to survive, no matter how.*

My hands scream of feeling the very light of my sanity begin to pour down a hideous vortex of blackness, and suddenly I rebel! I am not a beast! I am a man! I will be a man and I will have a past! With a tremendous effort I take back control of my hands, and they pound one last defiant chord, one mighty *harmonious* C-major chord, and at that instant, my mind splits wide open and I remember everything, every wonderful, every *horrible*, every *UNSPEAKABLE* thing.

I know who I am. I know what has happened to me. I remember the little flat in Ghent, where I taught piano, where I played Beethoven and Shostakovich on my old Bechstein grand, where Paul taught English, where we were happy. I remember how many times I'd thanked God that Paul was not there when the Nazis came, and how many times I'd cursed God that I *was* there. I remember praying that Paul would not try to find me, that Paul would escape to England.

I remember the cattle car filled with quicklime mixed with wounded bodies writhing in pain, like worms in a saltcellar. I remember the brief, desperate bondings among the damned, destined for those lethal showers. Again I know all my anger, all my horror, all my helpless outrage, and my final madness, my terrible, my complete madness, the dragons that filled my head, roiling and screaming in my head, drowning out the real world with their hideous screaming! I remember the desperation of pouring out that madness in the best language I could muster, and on any scraps of paper I could find in that hell-hole of a camp. Yes, now I remember finding those yellowed scraps of paper, and how I once poured out my maddened soul onto them.

I remember killing a man with my bare hands, with these very hands, and I remember my escape—barbed wire, running, brambles, a forest, barking dogs, mortal despair! Again I feel those dragons, writhing in my mind and striking now at my mouth. My mouth finds its voice at last, and I scream, and *I scream*, and *I SCREAM!* The last thing that I hear as my consciousness dies is my own terrified screaming.

But I awake, and I am alive. The forest is black and close and silent, and the baying of the dogs is gone, miraculously gone. I am cold and hungry and exhausted and lost and frightened and terribly alone. The forest is not a refuge, it is a prison. I have nowhere to go. I feel the terrible silence of the dark trees closing in on me, and again the dragons roil in my mind.

But one by one the trees rise up. One tree claps, and another, and suddenly the forest is applauding; the forest is crying out to me, cheering me, celebrating that I am alive, that I have somehow survived! Slowly I look around me, and the trees are people, and the people are the audience in the little hall, and they are cheering me, cheering my life and my survival!

Reality washes over me in waves. I am John Phillip Butler, and *I have my miracle!* I will play Beethoven again, and Shostakovich! I will sit safely at another old Bechstein, and my hands will sing again!

Tender arms are holding me, and I finally recognize Paul. Paul, the man with the sheets of music. Paul, resurrected from my long-lost memories. Paul, from the little flat in Ghent. Paul, the only man I ever really loved. Paul is telling me that I am safe, that it is over, that they can't hurt me now. Paul is telling me that he *did* escape, that a miracle has brought us back together, that my burned face and torn hands don't matter, that he loves me, that we can start over, *today*. And it's true. I am safe. I have my miracle. I have a future. *We* have a future. I am not screaming now. I am sobbing like a child.

Moira is there beside me and sobbing with me. She smiles through her tears and strokes my hands. "Look," she says softly, "They're at peace now." I look at my hands, and they lie still.

And silent.

The Incident of the Large Lady

Why yes, since you ask, I do believe that teleportation is possible. In fact, I believe that it happens, and when I've told you the incident of the Large Lady and the Microwave, I expect that you'll agree.

The Large Lady *wafted* into the break room with all that excessive grace that large ladies are wont to affect when they're in uncertain situations. You see, she was a temp on her first day. She knew nobody in the room, and nobody knew her. Her generous form was poured into a dress of green-on-white dotted Swiss, with the green duplicated in faux-emerald necklace and earrings. Her champagne-blond hair was pulled back tightly in a sort of *chignon*, and her simple pumps were of the same champagne hue. She smiled at the room's occupants but didn't speak.

She carried a Tupperware object and a Danielle Steel paperback romance. She placed the Tupperware in the communal microwave. This was before the microwave became a *de rigueur* kitchen appliance, and most of us still regarded the machine with some awe. The Large Lady punched several buttons and the machine hummed obediently. Then she pulled up a folding chair intimately close to the microwave, sat, and immersed herself in her Danielle Steel.

Now the microwave sat against a wall, and beyond that wall was a room that was being, in corporate-speak, *repurposed*. That is, it was being reconstructed from the ground up. Suddenly, from an invisible point exactly behind the microwave, a jackhammer sprang into thunderous action. Everybody in the break room jumped, but the Large Lady did something much more spectacular. She simply disappeared. Vanished. *Evaporated.*

Our hasty search found her a few minutes later in a nearby hallway, shaken and exhausted and clutching her Danielle Steel to her ample bosom. Witnesses in that hallway said that she had materialized there with the same jarring suddenness as her evaporation. People in the connecting hall said that she had not been seen to occupy any of that intervening space, even for an instant, though they admitted being distracted by the sudden noise of the jackhammer. We were left with an abiding conviction that she had teleported, or been teleported, from the break room to the point of her subsequent discovery.

Her overheated state and confusion were consistent with having been reassembled from elementary particles just moments before. Furthermore, she was never heard to deny our conclusion. As final evidence, one of the faux-emerald earrings was missing and never found, possibly thrown out of the transmission envelope during passage, and lost somewhere in a meta-space.

Obviously, the incident of the Large Lady had the potential to advance human knowledge in many fields: atomic physics, medicine, philosophy. One of our number, who happened to be entering graduate school at that very time, immediately shifted his research to an effort to reproduce what had happened to the Large Lady, but in the controlled environment of the laboratory. With the help of witnesses, he set up an apparatus that faithfully duplicated the break room microwave, the jackhammer, and the folding chair. To avoid the obvious ethical issues, the investigator replaced the Large Lady with an inanimate object, namely a copy of the same Danielle Steel paperback romance.

Not one of the hundreds of experiments duplicating the incident caused any change in the state of the Danielle Steel. Eventually it was decided that the assistance of the Large Lady herself would be required, if not as the subject of the experiment, then at least as a technical advisor.

Alas, the Large Lady, once she was tracked down and invited, turned the investigator down flat. Further attempts to entice her, enriched with generous honoraria, got no better results. Finally, a lawyer sent an official-looking brief saying that the Large Lady wished to put the incident behind her, and that the investigator should cease and desist. Thus was doomed the experiment that might have changed the fate of mankind.

So yes, I do believe that teleportation is possible. In fact, I believe that it happens, and after learning about the incident of the Large Lady and the Microwave, I expect that you agree.

In St. Peter's Square

I was there! After all these years, I still can't believe it, but I was there. I was only nineteen, but even I fully realized the importance of that moment. In the fifty years since then, mankind have walked on Mars and Titan, families can vacation on the Moon, and we have all but ended war and world hunger and homelessness. But it's still that day in Rome that sets my heart pounding and makes my knees weak.

A papal conclave is supposed to be a solemn moment, a time for meditation and prayer, but this was more like a carnival, except that people weren't really making merry. Instead, the atmosphere was one of anticipation and nervousness, as all of us there in St. Peter's Square knew the world could be changing under our feet. I had found something solid to stand on, so I had a good view of the crowd, and during the wait I made the acquaintance of a scholarly-looking gentleman who stood next to me. Andrew Butler was from San Francisco, and a well-known authority on all things Vatican.

Andy was happy to fill me in on just what was happening: "The College of Cardinals meets under Michelangelo's incredible frescoes in the Sistine Chapel, there just to the right of the Basilica of St. Peter. They're 'in conclave,' meaning under lock and key, until they've made their decision."

I thought that must be really problematic. "That could take a long time, couldn't it? A long time to be locked in one room. Are there toilets? How do they eat or sleep?"

Andy laughed. "Common misconception. Maybe it was that way once, but now they have all the conveniences. They aren't *literally* locked into the Chapel; they're escorted under guard among it and their dining hall, where they are very well fed, and they have private rooms with everything they might want—except communication devices."

"They're locked into a *group*," Andy explained, "A group that can have no communication with the outside world until they make their decision. No communication except that after each vote, they burn their ballots to keep them secret, and they add materials to color the smoke, black if no decision, white if they have decided. Traditionally, there are two votes each morning and two each afternoon. But even after they send up the white smoke there are still rites to be performed before the new pope can be presented to the public. It can be an hour or more before we see the senior cardinal appear on the balcony to greet the crowd and pronounce those traditional words, *Habemus Papam*, which means, of course, 'we have a pope.' And *then* we'll finally hear the name of the new Holy Father." Andy spoke precisely, like the academic that he was.

Every conclave is a great occasion, but this vote could be historic. Centuries of tradition, of dogma even, could be crumbling away, and the heavens could be opening on a new world, a world of blinding possibilities, of unheard-of promise, of uncharted seas. The news media had talked about half a dozen possibilities, but the experts had made it clear that there were only two candidates that the College of Cardinals would seriously consider: Antonio, the candidate for modernization, and Verdi, the candidate for tradition. I asked Andy for his prognosis.

"Oddsmakers heavily favor Verdi," Andy explained, "because the church seldom challenges its own traditions.

You see, Antonio is a layperson—that's anyone who's never been ordained a priest—and the last layperson elected pope was Leo X in 1513. Electing a layperson adds some complexity to the rites to be performed behind the scenes."

I raised my eyebrows, "Oh? Like what?"

Andy explained. "The usual procedure is that once the decision has been reached, the new pope is asked if they accept the position. Then the cardinals pay homage and vow obedience. Then the pope is fitted into new robes, which can take some time. Only then can the presentation take place." Andy paused to make sure I understood. I nodded, then asked, "So what else has to happen?"

"In the case of a lay person, there are several more steps. The candidate must be ordained a priest, then promoted to bishop, and then to cardinal. Each rite has to be performed entirely, but without an audience and without unnecessary pomp. Popular opinion holds that the cardinals find all that distasteful. It seems to interrupt the smooth flow of procedure that's been developed over so many centuries."

"So Antonio has little chance?" I asked, frowning. "Antonio is clearly the popular choice. Editorials and readers' posts in blogs all over the world have been debating this for weeks now, sometimes with vitriol. It seems clear to me that the popular movement to modernize the church is taking over the world. Of course, the princes of the church haven't joined in those debates. Everybody knows their conservative position." Andy nodded, and looked away thoughtfully.

This conclave could be a historic one, so the faithful of both camps had descended upon Rome. Whatever the cardinals' decision, people wanted to be there to celebrate their win or to mourn their loss, together with thousands of their fellow believers. Nonbelievers came just to watch history in the making. I was one of those. I wanted to see the reactions, to hear the cries of victory or defeat, to feel the rush of a pivotal point in history. I wanted to be able to say, "I was there!"

But first there was the waiting, the endless hours of waiting. At first the crowd was calm and well behaved, reverent, as befitted the occasion. Only carefully screened persons are admitted to the square during a conclave, and a substantial security force monitors the ungated entrance and the crowd. But this time was different. The crowd outside the square grew in size and vigor until it surged through the security guard and streamed into the square. The authorities made a brave attempt to limit the numbers, but eventually they accepted the inevitable. Everyone found the tightly packed crowd and the disorder unseemly, but the alternative—ploughing the faithful out of the square—was unthinkable. There would probably be injuries, and possibly ugly international incidents. Security was provided not by the Vatican or Roman police, but by the Italian State Police, and they were sensitive to the delicate position that protecting Vatican City put them in. Andy explained all of this to me during the endless waiting.

As the hours passed, the emotions of the crowd swelled until stillness and silence were no longer possible. People began to sing softly, and to sway in cadence. The crowd was so thick that it swayed as a single entity; no person could move independently.

In the swaying and singing, names were muttered, and knots began to form as people debated, shared rumors, and called out the names of their favorites. Then someone called out "smoke!" and then someone else, and soon everybody was pointing and crying out, "Smoke!" *"Fumo!"* *"Rauch!"* People stood on tiptoe and strained to see; children climbed onto their parent's shoulders.

The black smoke of indecision was met with a collective groan of disappointment. After an hour that felt like an eternity, there was a flutter from the chimney. Smoke? The crowd held their breath. No, it was a bird. A sigh, then another wait. More small talk with Andy.

Then another flutter from the chimney and again the crowd held its breath. White smoke! A decision! The crowd roared in anticipation. There was no singing now, only the cries of thousands of voices not yet sure whether to rejoice or despair, as they waited for the announcement.

But hours passed, and the shouting and singing gradually returned. Andy and I were both tired, and we both sat down on the box I'd been standing on. I was young and impatient, so I kept checking my watch. Andy noticed and said, "A long wait lends credence to the notion that a layperson has been chosen. Remember that there's more to be done in that case." That idea re-animated me a bit. Andy and I found things to talk about to pass the time. I learned more about the operation of the Vatican that day than all of what I'd known before.

Finally, the doors opened and a scarlet-clad cardinal emerged onto the balcony. As the cardinal's hands raised, a silence reverberated, as if his hands had suddenly lifted from holding a mighty chord on some great cosmic organ. And in the silence, every ear strained to hear the message. Slowly and solemnly, the cardinal delivered the greeting and pronounced those words that changed history.

There was a split second of silence after the last syllable was uttered, as people's brains assured them their ears had heard correctly. Then the world erupted into such an explosion of emotions as had never been witnessed: some shrieked and fainted; some cried and hugged; some cheered and clapped; some fell to their knees and bowed their heads, or raised their hands and faces to heaven in prayer. Some just stood in stunned silence, and I was one of those. I was so awed that I was right there as history was made that I couldn't act or speak. I knew that all over the world, people crowded around their viewing screens were right there with us there in St. Peter's Square.

And then there was another sound, a bell, many bells, thousands of bells in hundreds of towers. All the bells of Rome sang out in a great and growing cacophony. And around the world, church bells joined in. Many rang in joy and hope, some in alarm, and a few solemnly tolled in recognition of the passing of an era.

My legs still grow weak and my eyes teary as I recall those solemn words that mankind had waited so long to hear: "Habemus Papam. I announce to you a great joy: We have a pope! The Very Reverend Lucia Antonio of the Holy Church, who takes for herself the name of Maria."

Pope Maria I reigned for thirty-seven years. Under her moral leadership, the nations came together and ushered in an era of world peace and prosperity, the period now known as *Pax Maria.*

And when she was elevated, *I was there!*

Persimmon Road

— Maggie and Dan —

I remember that horse," Maggie mused, as she and Dan snuggled in the porch swing of the crumbling old house on Persimmon Road. "I remember that big chestnut stallion you rode around all over the county." She caressed Dan's thin gray hair. "Your hair was chestnut colored too, just like his mane. When you were ridin' up on the ridge, with your hair and his mane just streamin' in the wind, you looked like a couple-a gods or somethin'. You even wore chestnut-colored ridin' boots. And when you rode, sometimes you commenced singin', and these piney woods just rang with that big voice of yours." Her eyes, old and sunken as they were, still sparkled at the memory. "All the girls thought Ada must be just the luckiest girl in the county to be your wife. Oh yes, I remember that." Maggie's face was leathery and lined, and her toothless mouth was stained with snuff. She had aged and roughened into the very stereotype of a crone in an unwashed feedbag frock. Her long stringy hair was white, but with that sickly yellow cast that made old ladies of fashion rinse with laundry bluing.

"That was a long time ago," Dan replied, "An awful long time ago. You were something to see yourself. Who would have thought we'd all end up old wrecks like this?" He kicked the floor gently and the old chain-hung porch swing creaked into a wider arc.

"Or dead," Maggie looked up at him. "We're about all

50

that's left, Dan, and we're fallin' apart like this old house. Look at those old shutters danglin' there, and those clapboards all curlin' up like that. They say the full moon pulls the nails out at night. You reckon so?"

"Probably not; it's just an old tale. But old tales can be a comfort sometimes. Doesn't matter whether they're true." Dan's hand caressed Maggie's cheek as though she were a beauty queen. He was old too, but a little more presentable, with a Roman nose and a body that still remembered its powerful build in youth. He pulled Maggie close in his arms and began to softly sing a song from their childhood:

> *I wandered today to the hill, Maggie*
> *To watch the scene below*
> *The creek and the old rusty mill, Maggie*
> *Where we sat in the long, long ago*

The house, built in the antebellum Tidewater Farmhouse style, mirrored their age. It was a big house, a two-story house, with wide verandas all around. The shutters were askew or missing entirely, and of the veranda bannisters, only enough survived to barely support the railing. The house had been innocent of paint for decades, and the only evidence that it had once been white was the fact that all Tidewater Farmhouses had started life white. It sat high up on many solid brick pillars, safe from the occasional storm surges that gave the architectural style its name. Persimmon Road was not a flood zone, but the house's builders had adhered to a style, because that was what builders did.

> *And now we are aged and gray, Maggie,*
> *And the trials of life nearly done;*
> *But to me you're as fair as you were, Maggie*
> *When you and I were young*

A few hens of uncertain pedigree scratched in the sand spread among ancient pecan and live oak trees in the big yard. It was an old-fashioned yard, from the days when carefully maintained white river sand stood in for today's green lawn. A lone black Jersey milk cow chewed her cud contentedly in the shade of one gnarled apple tree, the sole survivor of a ruined orchard. Maggie regarded the scrawny bird dogs napping among the terraced surface roots of the largest oak. "I wonder if we could teach them dogs to hunt foxes."

Dan choked. It was a silly notion, but that didn't matter. Maggie *understood*.

— Louise —

It was a lazy, bucolic scene, one that could have been from 1900, even earlier. But then a pink Nash sedan turned in from Persimmon Road, and it was clearly 1955. "Louise is here," Maggie sighed. "I better go pick some beans or somethin."

"Father, dear father, come home with me now!" Dan quoted. "I wonder if she has something to say today that she hasn't already said at least a dozen times."

Louise strode from the Nash to the porch with the determined gait of a middle-aged schoolmarm bent on disciplining a rowdy charge. It turned out that she had thought of something new to say, but first she repeated all the old things. Dan couldn't stay with Maggie. It was scandalous. He had to come home with Louise. What were people saying? Besides, Maggie was dirty and smelly and had no teeth. Her house had no plumbing, and it was full of flies. Nobody had even been upstairs in recent memory, and the rooms up there must be in a scandalous, unsanitary state. The outhouse was probably full of black widow spiders, not to mention the occasional copperhead. Finally, she played rísh

her new card. "And that wagon! I hear that you go out on the highway in that wagon with that mule! You're gonna get killed, Papa!"

"Now Louise," Dan replied patiently, "State law still gives farm wagons the right of way. I know it won't be that way much longer, but right now, we have the right to drive that wagon on the highway, and everybody else has to respect that right. We're never in any hurry to get anyplace. That's one of the things I hate about today—everybody's always rushing around, even when they don't know why."

"But Papa, half the traffic on that highway is New Yorkers hell-bent to get to Florida. They don't know state laws—they don't even know what state they're in most of the time. For them it's just New York and Florida and a road in between. And they have those big, heavy cars! Oh, Papa, I'm scared, really *scared*!" Louise was almost crying.

Dan took her in his arms in a fatherly embrace. "It's gonna be alright, Honey. This house may not be what you want for me, but it's what I want. Everything here is like it was in the house where I grew up." Dan tilted his daughter's chin up to his face. "Maggie is the only one left who remembers. She's like me, Louise, like me. Your house is fine, but it belongs to a different world, a world where everything smells of Oxydol and canned soup. I visited in that world for a while, and I appreciate all you did for me, but I belong in this one. Here, it's like two world wars and television never happened.

"Maggie may not be the housekeeper you are, honey, but this house is not filthy. We do a little cleaning every day. I've been upstairs. It's mighty dusty up there, but there's nothing worse than that—just dust. You mustn't begrudge an old man his last chance to feel like he belongs. Now, we've been over all this stuff too many times, and I want you to be brave and trust your Papa. I've lived all this long and never even broken a bone. I must be doing something right. You've got a family of your own to worry about. You take care of Michael and Bonnie, and don't you worry about me."

Louise didn't take defeat willingly, but she did eventually retreat. She started her car, but for a while, she just sat there with her hands on the wheel. "She's like me," Dan had said. Oh, why did those words sound so foreboding? Yes, *yes*, it was what Ashley had told Scarlett about Melanie! "She's like me, Scarlett," he had said. Oh, what heartbreak Ashley might have spared everybody if he had just married Scarlett instead of Melanie! Maybe there'd never even have been a war! Louise shook her head. This was crazy thinking; *Gone With the Wind* was just a novel. Besides, her foot had grown light on the clutch, and the Nash was straining to go home.

Maggie walked back to the house with a battered peck bucket full of garden produce. "I got roas'n' ears for supper," she said. "You stayin'?"

"As long as you'll have me, Maggie Everett."

"As long as I'm still breathin', Dan Mills." Maggie set down her bucket. Dan took her into his arms, and they stood there, just holding each other, for a long time.

— The Crash —

Louise's fears did not prove ungrounded, but when Nemesis came, she was not a Yankee in a Florida-bound Roadmaster. She was Laes Andersen in Jim Johnson's big Pure Oil tanker truck.

It was a Tuesday morning, the fifth of July. Rockfish County celebrated the Fourth in a big way, and Laes had been carousing pretty much all night. Maybe he wasn't still drunk, but he did have one righteous hangover. There'd been no gas deliveries for three days, so all the stations would be running low. Jim had told Laes to get started early and cover lots of ground, and Laes was doing his best to do just that.

So when he rounded the curve just before the Rockfish Creek narrow one-lane bridge and spied Maggie's mule-drawn wagon clopping along ahead, he just overreacted. The tanker jackknifed and swung around into a big V that swept up all in its path, including the heavy concrete sidewalls of the bridge. Maggie and Dan were right in that V, so they were pretty much in the middle of the fireball, when it bloomed. They can't have suffered.

Laes' driver's door was on the outside of the V, and he was able to jump to safety and suffer no more than a sprained ankle. He had enough sense to know that this was a thing that there was no use trying to run away from, so he sat down on the red clay ditch bank, cradled his aching head, and chain-smoked Chesterfields until the authorities came. That didn't take long. You could see the greasy black smoke all the way to the County Seat.

For the first time in many years, the house on Persimmon Road spent the night sad and alone. Nobody lit the kerosene lanterns. Nobody fed the cow or the chickens. Nobody climbed into the big bed, the one with its feather mattress almost at hip height, in the Victorian fashion. Come dawn, nobody milked the cow, though she stood at the barn door and lowed softly, as if asking for relief. But old Bony McGowan, who had sharecropped Maggie's land for many years, heard the news and came to the animals' rescue. He simply added their care to the list of tasks that he already always did around Maggie's place. He entered the house only to close the windows and doors, preparing the house for a long, lonely period of silence.

— Laes —

Laes Andersen was not born in Rockfish County. Just out of the army, he'd drifted through, looking for cheap beer and cheap women. Apparently, there were plenty of both in Rockfish County if you knew what rocks to turn over, and if there's anything the army teaches a man, it's how to find those rocks. Laes would probably have drifted on eventually, but Jim Johnson took a shine to him and gave him a job driving his tanker. Anita had been an Andersen, though no relation to Laes, before Jim married her. She'd given him twin girls, but she'd died doing it. Maybe Laes was the son she and Jim never had. At any rate, Laes drifted into Rockfish County and he didn't drift out.

Laes was one of the most loved, most hated, most feared, and most talked-about men in the county. But no matter how much folks talked about him, nobody ever really said why. Nobody ever said it out loud, but Laes Andersen was drop-dead gorgeous. He had a swimmer's body and a soldier's bearing. His chiseled face included sky-blue eyes that looked right through you, and saw your every secret, and didn't care. His smile was endearing, his movements smooth and catlike. He wore tight Levis and tight sleeveless T-shirts that showed off every nuance of his body. He rode a big Indian Chief motorcycle, and when the wind tossed his wavy blond hair, it fell back maddeningly in place. Everything about Laes seemed perfect, at least to look at, but he had the reputation of a libertine.

Wherever farm wives gathered on a selected back porch to shell aprons full of peas for supper, Laes' name was bound to come up. If ever it came out that some farm girl would be spending time ministering to a maiden aunt in a distant town, Laes would be the prime suspect.

Teenage girls idolized Laes and dreamed of playing

Scarlett to his Rhett. Teenage boys admired and hated him and dreamed of playing Robin to his Batman. Parents simply feared him.

Burt Cartwright, who owned the Texaco by the railroad tracks and cut hair on the side, pretty much summed up the way fathers felt when he said to his customer, "George, why would a man like that even want to be good? Do you want a little more off the top?"

Amanda Murphy probably represented most of the mothers' views when she counseled her daughter, "June, a man like Laes can't be true to one woman, no matter how much he wants to. There are just too many other women who will always want a piece of him." June Murphy saw the longing in her mother's eyes, and she knew that epiphany, which for most girls comes too late, if ever. After that, Amanda was not just June's mother; she was her friend.

Sheriff Booger Blake shared the general distrust of Laes, and he was more than happy to slap him into the county slammer. Then he sat down and made a list of every possible charge that he might bring. He grinned to his deputy, "This oughta keep him outta trouble for a long, long time."

— Charles —

Louise went into a state of shock, and it was left to her brother Joel to make the arrangements. It was obvious that what had been recovered of Dan should be buried in the family plot in the cemetery at tiny Hope Springs Church. It was not at all obvious what to do with Maggie, but since she had no known relatives, Joel took responsibility for her remains as well. He suggested laying Dan where his late wife Ada would lie at his right side, and then laying Maggie on his left.

Louise was scandalized. "You'd put that... that creature near my Mama?" she shrieked. "Don't you even think? What would people say? What would Mama do on resurrection morning? I just don't believe you!" A little later, and a bit calmer, she actually had a constructive suggestion. "She belongs beside Charles," she said. "Find out where he is, and we'll go from there."

It had been sixty years since Charles Everett had bought the antebellum house on Persimmon Road and brought his new bride there to be its mistress. Sixty years since Charles had marched away to serve his country, never to return. Sixty years that Maggie had lived alone, cloistered in her unchanging world, fading from a youthful Southern belle into the ruined crone whose very antiquity had drawn Dan to her side. Sixty years that the old house had deteriorated, needed only by one ancient being who hardly left the two rooms that she used.

Most people had forgotten Charles long ago, but Louise knew that there had been such a man, and that he must be buried somewhere. So Joel did the research and came back to report that Charles lay in Havana Harbor, one of nine bodies never recovered from the explosion of the *Maine*, and that Maggie could not join him there. "Look, Sis, she was once a lady, the wife of a kind of hero. The *Maine* got us into the Spanish American War, the war that turned America from a country into an empire. There's history here. What you saw was not the real Maggie, just a fossil made by time and fate. She made your Papa happy at a time when nobody else in the whole world could do that. Don't you think he deserves to have her beside him now?"

Louise fell limply into a chair. "All right, Joel. Go ahead and do it. You're probably right. And anyway, I'm just too tired to care anymore."

— Rev. Paul Clark —

So it was that on one of those fine summer mornings when mockingbirds sing bright melodies and bees hum a soft drone bass, Dan's friends and family gathered at Hope Springs to lay him and Maggie to rest together. The Reverend Paul Clark said a few words meant to comfort the bereaved. "They were two souls lost in a world that they didn't understand," he said, "a world that no longer understood them. They did not belong here, so the Lord prepared a great chariot of fire to take those two lost souls to where they do belong."

Louise had not thought of it in just that way, and somehow the idea gave her some comfort. But then the Reverend continued, "And the Lord prepared a charioteer..." and all comfort was gone. Louise blamed herself; she blamed Maggie; she blamed nearly everybody; but most of all she blamed Laes Andersen, and to suggest that he was in any way an instrument of the Lord's will was intolerable. She leaped up and tried to shout a protest. Luckily, she was completely incoherent, and Joel only had to grab her sleeve to pull her back down into the pew, where she landed in a sobbing heap. Most people in the little chapel never even knew that anything untoward had happened.

Laes's crash was the event of the decade, and the *Rockfish County Chronicle* reported every available detail. Thus, the Reverend's words eventually reached a much-subdued Laes Andersen in the county jail. "Jim, what do you think about what that preacher said?" he asked Jim Johnson when he came to bring fresh Chesterfields.

"Well, I don't know much about how the Lord works," Jim answered. "But I do reckon that things happen for a reason; some things, anyway. I think it's what you think about it that matters, don't you?"

— Sarah —

Later, Sarah Chalmers, the lone *Chronicle* reporter, interviewed Laes in jail. "I expected to find a reckless playboy," she reported. "Instead I found a thoughtful, sober man genuinely concerned with how he could repay the community for his conduct."

So began a metamorphosis, one that played out in the pages of the *Chronicle* and that every citizen of Rockfish County watched closely. Sarah Chalmers was intrigued by this strange chameleon of a man, and she made it her special project to uncover his mysteries. Her *Chronicle* articles gradually revealed a man nobody expected. A well-bred, well-educated, well-read man. A man who had never fathered a child, in Rockfish County or anywhere else. Sarah researched that point very carefully, and she found that every suspect pregnancy in the county since Laes's arrival was definitely the work of someone else.

"Why on earth did you never try to quash all those rumors?" she asked.

"Well," Laes replied, "I believed the advice given to George Minifer, I think by his uncle George Amberson, 'Gossip is never fatal until it is denied.'"

"You've read Tarkington?" Sarah gasped.

"I've read just about everybody, Sarah. There wasn't much else to do when I was a kid. I was a wallflower until I enlisted in the army. The army changed me, and I suddenly admitted to all that pent-up need. When I got out, I just needed to let off some steam. I know now that was a big mistake, and I'm ready to do whatever it takes to make up for it. I'm not a religious man, but I do believe in karma and redemption."

— Arnold —

Unlike most of Rockfish County, Louise read Sarah's *Chronicle* articles with exasperation. "How can she be so naïve?" she complained to her husband, Michael. "That man's a con—how can she not see that? She's just letting him sweep her off her feet like any other floozy." Louise wrote several letters to the editor in this vein and was surprised to see a dozen or so responses from the community, all disagreeing with her, some quite nastily. "Michael," she lamented, "that man killed my father! How can everybody take his side? I don't understand it. What's going on? What am I missing?"

Michael was cautious. "I'm not part of this, Louise, but I think you should go see him in jail and find out for yourself."

Louise was flabbergasted. "I couldn't do that! What would it look like? Besides, I'd be in tears, or I'd be too mad to talk. I'm just not ready for anything like that. Not ready at all."

In a week's time, Louise was ready. "Well, I'm going. I'm probably crazy, but I've got to know. I'm going." She made her appointment with the county jail, put on mourning, cranked the Nash, and went.

Laes was taken aback when a warden opened his cell door and ushered Louise in. For a few minutes, both stumbled over embarrassed tongues, but slowly they organized around familiar roles. Louise was a schoolmarm, and here was a naughty but penitent boy. Laes was a soldier, and here was a superior officer. After some awkward preliminaries, Laes summarized, "As for explaining myself, I have no excuse. Sure, I have reasons, but no reason that I can call an excuse."

Louise felt curiosity edging out her anger and grief. "Can you tell me about those reasons? The ones that aren't an excuse? What do you mean by that?"

"It's about how men react to surviving near-death experiences, Louise. You see, in Korea every patrol was a near-death experience. We knew we were sitting ducks, there were enemies hiding everywhere, more than ready to pick us off. Every moment was like my last, until I was back in camp. The stress was awful!

"Whenever I got back to a safe place, and breathed my first good deep breath, I'd go a little bit crazy. I was alive! I had to celebrate that I was a man, and alive. We all felt that way, and we all let off steam however we could. Some guys just yelled; some drank; some sang; but most headed for the nearest brothel. When a man needs to reassure himself that he is a man and alive, sex is what does it. It's way ahead of whatever is in second place. You tell yourself, 'I'm a new man! Let's see what I can do!' And a raw display of virility is what does it for you. You can read up on this, because it's already being studied by academic types."

Louise stared straight ahead. This was touching a raw nerve. "Well, I wasn't in that safe place very often, so Korea was just one long near-death experience. I built up a lot of pressure. When I was finally discharged, I bought a big motorcycle and headed out to see the country, and when I got here a couple of days later, I was still bursting with that pent-up need. Apparently, women like me, because I had more offers than I could take. It was what I needed, and I found myself rutting like a March hare. I don't apologize for that; it was probably just what I was supposed to do, under the circumstances, but it went on too long. I should have gotten it out of my system and started acting like a grown man, but I didn't. I let myself get used to it, and I made it a lifestyle for several years. That was a mistake. Louise, what's wrong? Did I say too much? Are you okay?"

Louise was staring into space, her face wracked by deep anguish. Laes jumped up to call a guard, but Louise grabbed his arm with a trembling hand and pulled him back down.

"I've been here before," she quavered. "I've tried to forget it, but I've had this talk before. Only it was my boy, my boy Arnold. He was just back, and I thought he was running wild. I called him on it, and he told me just what you just said." Louise was crying now. "I told him as long as he was under my roof he'd live by my rules, and when I got up the next morning he was gone. Gone! He never said goodbye, and he never called, and he never wrote, and I don't know where he is, or if he's OK. Laes, I drove him away! I drove my boy away because I couldn't see that he was a man; he'd been through hell and he needed to be a man, and I was just a woman who couldn't understand; who *wouldn't* understand. I was *wrong*, Laes, so *wrong!*" Louise collapsed against Laes, and he just held her while she cried herself dry.

When Louise had exhausted herself and found some rationality, she told Laes that her daughter Bonnie believed Arnold was in San Francisco, "but she won't say how she knows." Laes promised to ask an old army buddy there to look for Arnold. They parted friends.

Later, as Louise drove the Nash home, she stopped at Jiffy DoNut and bought a baker's dozen glazed. She went home, made coffee, and ate them all. Then she sat at her typewriter and composed a letter to the *Chronicle*, a letter of a very different sort.

And a few weeks later, Arnold called. Laes's buddy had found him and delivered Louise's message. Arnold was established in San Francisco, and he would stay there, but the rift in the family was mended. Now, Louise had two sons, because Laes had worked a miracle, and he would be a part of the newly mended family from now on.

Laes's notoriety slowly turned into fame, and distrust grew into admiration. When the lawyer that Jim Johnson hired for Laes went back to once again plead for bail, the judge, who had flatly refused to consider bail for a libertine with no local ties, simply released Laes into the custody of Jim Johnson.

By the time Laes came to trial, there was no doubt as to the outcome. Even Louise went to bat for him. Finally, there was a motion to dismiss, and the motion was granted. Laes Andersen was a free man again, a sadder and a wiser man, but a free man.

— Bonnie —

Since Maggie had neither will nor relatives, her land and house on Persimmon Road eventually wound up on the auction block. Jim Johnson had plans for that place. Maybe he had always dreamed that his relationship with Laes would somehow grow into a paternal one, that Laes would someday be the son to inherit Jim's gas and oil business. Maybe the crisis of the crashed tanker jolted Jim into the realization that he couldn't just wait for all that to happen, that he needed to work toward those dreams, and that turning Laes into a stable citizen, a landed citizen, was the first step. Whatever his reasons, he called in a lot of markers all over the county to make sure nobody bid at that auction. On auction day there was only one bid, and Laes Andersen bought Maggie's place for about the price of a nice new Cadillac. He borrowed the money from Jim Johnson.

Laes moved into the house right away and devoted all his energies to cleaning and fixing it. He still drove for Jim, making enough money to keep food in the house. Money for building supplies came from old Boney McGowan, who kept on sharecropping the land for Laes.

Laes was a natural fixer, and he already had the building skills he needed. As the years passed, he wired the house and outbuildings, and added modern indoor plumbing. He replaced the shake roof with the standing-seam steel that was popular for farmhouses then. Over the years, he put in central heat and air conditioning, and a modern kitchen and bathrooms.

Laes didn't know anything at all about decorating, but as it happened, Louise's daughter Bonnie did. Bonnie was a plain girl, a practical girl, the kind of girl who wasted no time bemoaning her fate or planning a fancy dress for the prom that she knew she would attend alone. She wore her plain brown hair in a simple boyish bob and used makeup sparingly. When she could, she wore dungarees and a plaid shirt. Now she was studying interior design at nearby Cavette College, and she needed a term project. The house on Persimmon Road was perfect.

The house dated from antebellum times. It had been fairly ordinary when it was built, but a century had passed. Time had changed values, and Maggie's simple lifestyle had preserved some things that were simply not seen in new houses, or even in most old ones. "Your house can be like a museum, Laes," Bonnie explained. "Look at all this woodwork! All native oak! Lucky for you! Most of the local oak is just gone now, and if people bother with woodwork at all they just use pine. Back then people wanted dark mahogany, but if they couldn't afford it, they settled for stained oak. We can strip it all and finish it natural. With less stain it'll suit today's tastes just fine. You'll have something unique in the whole county."

There were little treasures, sometimes big ones, constantly turning up. A box of photographs of Charles and Maggie, including one showing Charles playing an old square piano, and some ancient daguerreotypes of persons unknown. Art Nouveau paintings. An 1898 "Remember the Maine" poster. Some really fine antique furniture pieces. And shoved under the staircase, a square piano, apparently the very one in the photograph, still containing several nineteenth-century songbooks. "Chickering!" Bonnie exclaimed. "You couldn't get much better than that at the time! That Charles was no slouch! It hasn't been opened for decades, and inside it's like new!" Bonnie gasped as Laes stumbled through the first few measures of a Chopin etude. "You play!"

Laes grinned. "I wasn't always a wastrel, Bonnie."

Bonnie easily infected Laes with her enthusiasm, and soon the two of them were stripping and sanding and mending and shellacking like two kids in a sandbox. Bonnie sang as she worked, and Laes started joining in, in harmony. They started switching parts on an agreed signal from either, and they found that they were good at that kind of cooperation. It grew into a camaraderie that made the work fast and fun. So finally, at the moment when all the wainscoting and banisters were finally done, when Bonnie had cleaned the last brush and Laes had hammered the lid back on the last can, they stood back and admired their work for only a moment. Then they grabbed each other and danced.

So nobody was really surprised when the *Chronicle* reported that Michael and Louise Arden announced the engagement of their daughter Bonnie to Mr. Laes Anderson of Persimmon Road. Some people were jealous; some were disappointed; maybe some were even angry; but nobody was surprised.

— Today —

It has been one hundred and ten years now since Charles Everett bought the house on Persimmon Road, and fifty years since Laes crashed Jim Johnson's tanker. That tanker has grown into a small fleet, each bearing the signage "Andersen Oil."

The pavements and curbs of the town have snaked out into the countryside and crept up Persimmon Road. Out where Persimmon meets the highway, Chubb's family store has grown into a Piggly Wiggly that covers a city block. Boney McGowan's acres of green corn and alfalfa have grown into Everett Estates, rows of neat tract houses surrounding a manicured golf course. In the clubhouse, a display case holds those photos of Charles and Maggie and that authentic "Remember the Maine" poster.

Maggie's antebellum farmhouse, ordinary by the standards of its time, is now a mansion and a virtual museum. Everett House sits regally on three acres of land in the middle of the subdivision, like a queen holding court among her common subjects. The exterior is once again brightly white, with green shutters and trim. The original oak and pecan trees have grown into astounding giants, and a repopulated fruit orchard once again yields a generous harvest of quality fruits. Maggie's garden, now tilled lovingly for all these years, yields roasting ears, tomatoes, and many other delights for the Anderson table.

Inside, the house exudes happiness. The rooms mix antebellum splendor with modern convenience. The rooms are large, with high ceilings sporting crown molding and chandelier roses. There is polished chair rail, with oak wainscoting below and hand-painted wallpaper above. The large windows come nearly to the floors, so the antique sofas sit away from the walls in the nineteenth-century fashion. The stair is wide, with carved banisters and a balustrade wide enough to invite children to slide down it.

And children there are. Four generations of Andersens gather here regularly to celebrate holidays and family occasions. Every few years, Laes gathers those who have not heard the story before and tells them, in simple terms that children can understand, the tale of Maggie and Dan, how they died, and how that led to Laes's own redemption from a life of dissipation. It's not a happy tale, but it has to be told, because family secrets of this sort can fester and become traumas. Laes is determined that that won't happen in the Andersen family.

Rockfish County still celebrates the Fourth of July in a big way. The Everett Estates clubhouse sponsors its own fireworks display, and the extended Andersen family is always there to join the celebration.

But a more important rite happens the next day, on the fifth of July, when all the Andersen children, grandchildren, and great-grandchildren have dispersed to their own homes. Laes and Bonnie sit together at the old Chickering and sing the old songs from the old songbooks. The old house seems to put on a nostalgic smile as they sing a favorite:

> *The green grove is gone from the hill, Maggie*
> *Where first the daisies sprung;*
> *The creaking old mill is still, Maggie,*
> *Since you and I were young*

Then they raise a glass to that fifth of July so long ago, when the Lord prepared a great chariot of fire to gather *three* lost souls and take them to where they belonged.

Cherry Is Awesome

Gee, is that a tape recorder? I don't think I've ever talked into a tape recorder before. Daddy says when he was little, they used tape recorders, but I didn't know anybody still does now that we have digital stuff. Now everybody just uses their phone or their computer. In school we use an iPad. I'm in Miss Walters' fourth-grade class, you know, and I'm a *good* student. When I play with the iPad—okay, okay, don't have a cow. I'll talk.But don't forget you promised me ice cream. Do you think I can get cherry? Cherry is awesome!

My name first, right? I'm Benny Lewis, I'm nine years old, and I live in Rockport, and I'm supposed to tell you everything that happened yesterday afternoon—okay.

Suzy—that's my kid sister—Suzy and I were in the kitchen and I was making us some peanut butter sandwiches. I'd just got home from school, you know, and Aunt Val had just dropped Suzy off from kindergarten. She's not in real school yet you know. She's just five. Anyway, I was making these peanut butter sandwiches for us when Daddy got home. They weren't gonna be very good sandwiches, because I couldn't find any real bread. Just that whole-wheat stuff, you know. Daddy says it's good for us, but I don't like it. You can't taste the peanut butter. Well, unless you put an awful lot on. And why does everything have to be good for us, anyway? Oh, okay—yesterday afternoon. Don't have a cow, okay?

It was kinda chilly, so I lit the gas log. You just push a button, you know, so Daddy lets me light it. Then Daddy came in and he was really upset over something. He called me Benjamin, and he never calls me Benjamin unless I've done something awful, or something awful is wrong. Like when I threw the baseball through the big picture window just before the big rain came. Have you ever tried to sop a carpet dry with bath towels? With the rain still coming in? And working around all that glass? Oh, don't have a cow!

Anyway, Daddy was really upset. I asked him what was wrong, and he said he got his test back and he was clean. That didn't sound like something to be upset about to me, but I don't always understand grownups. Then Daddy took Mama's picture off the mantlepiece and he broke it in two over his knee and threw it into the fire, glass and all. That was weird, because he always tells me and Suzy that it's not a real fireplace and not to throw anything in it to burn. But he threw the picture right in.

Daddy's been upset a lot lately. You know Mama died last year—she was in a big wreck—and now Suzy's got this awful disease. It's got some name I can't ever remember, so I just call it awfulitis. I don't know anybody else at all who has it—well, Doc Lee did. You remember Doc Lee—he was the dentist before that new dentist came. I guess Doc Lee had this awfulitis thing and he didn't get it treated and he died. Anyway, Doc Mebane says it's good that he caught it early with Suzy, so he can treat it. Suzy's taking medicine and she's gonna be okay.

But yesterday, Daddy was even more upset than usual. Finally, he told me something like, "Benjamin, take Suzanne out and push her on the swing. *Now.*" It was kinda scary how upset he was, so I left the peanut butter sandwiches right there on the counter and took Suzy out. They weren't gonna be that good anyway. The sandwiches, I mean. Because I couldn't find any real bread. Okay, okay! Yesterday afternoon!

As we were going out, I could hear Daddy calling Aunt Val on the phone in his office. He was really upset, because he called her Valeria. He never calls her Valeria unless something is really wrong. Anyway, he was saying something like "Valeria, get over here right now. I need you here and I need you now." I think he even said something like "I'll never ask you for anything else again, just get over here now!"

So, I put Suzy in the swing and started pushing her. It was boring, boring! Do you know how boring it is to push a swing for a kid? I mean what's in it for you? She gets all the fun and all you get is tired. Daddy always tells me that a big brother is supposed to want to give his little sister fun, and someday I'll learn that it's fun just to see her having fun. I think that's some kind of grown-up trick, don't you? I mean if it's so much fun to push a swing, why don't the grown-ups do it themselves? Why make us kids do it? Don't they know we have stuff to do ourselves? Oh stop it. Okay. Don't have a cow. Back to yesterday afternoon. But you promised me ice cream, and don't you forget it.

Anyway, Aunt Val drove up real fast—I guess she didn't even get home before Daddy called her—and she pulled into the carport in the back. Our carport faces the alley, you know, not the street. She ran right past the swings and into the house without even saying hello. I guess she was pretty upset too. Then she started screaming and she didn't stop screaming. I thought I'd better go in, but just then she came running out. She was screaming and tearing at her hair and jumping around like some kind of monkey. When she saw me, she yelled something like "Benny, keep pushing that swing!" So I went back to pushing. I know when I'd better do what grown-ups say do, and this was one of those times. Aunt Val was using her phone with one hand and messing up her hair with the other.

Next thing I knew there was all this noise out front. I couldn't see what was going on, but people were shouting and there were sirens and stuff. Then Uncle Hamp pulled into the carport. I guess Aunt Val must have called him. He grabbed me and Suzy and stuffed us into his stupid little car and drove us off to their house. He has this little blue car he's so proud of. He calls it an original Mustang, and he thinks it's just so cool. Actually, it's little and old and dumpy, and it doesn't have any power at all. And the back seat is so little that Suzy fills it up, and she's just a little kid. Why would anybody get so worked up over such a dumpy little car? OKAY! Don't have a cow!

Anyway, I told Uncle Hamp I'd left two peanut butter sandwiches back home, so he made us two more. And he had real bread. And jelly. Daddy won't let us have jelly. He says jelly is bad for kids. I told Uncle Hamp how upset Daddy had been, and he said maybe we should spend the night with him and Aunt Val. I told him I'd have to see if it was okay with Daddy, but he said Aunt Val had already taken care of that, and we could sleep in Cousin Harry's room. Cousin Harry is all grown up and off at college, so nobody uses his room much. It's full of neat stuff, like posters of Madonna. There's a funny yellow poster of San Francisco with a funny airplane labeled "Jefferson Airplane" that Uncle Hamp says is collectible. I didn't get a chance to ask him what that means. I mean, anybody can collect anything, can't they? Do you need somebody's permission to collect a poster? Daddy used to collect stamps, and… Okay, okay! Yesterday afternoon!

Anyway, Uncle Hamp wanted to know what Daddy had said, too. So I told him how when Daddy first came home, he was asking me about when Mama had her root canals done. I don't know what he thought I'd remember about

Mama's going to Doc Lee for root canals. I mean I was just a little kid then, younger even than Suzy is now, and Suzy wasn't even born yet. And I had to stay with Aunt Val while Mama went to Doc Lee. What would I remember about Mama's root canals?

But I did remember when Suzy went to Doc Lee to have her baby teeth checked. I asked Daddy if he thought Suzy caught the awfulitis thing from Doc Lee when he was working on her baby teeth, but he said it wasn't something you caught, it was something you inherited if both your parents carried it. And you know? I think he was crying. I don't think I've seen Daddy cry since Mama died.

Anyway, that's everything that happened yesterday afternoon. Can I have that ice cream now? Do you think I can get cherry? Cherry is awesome!

Old American Customs
A Modern Greek Tragedy

Mom always did like you best, when we were kids. But that was okay, because I was Dad's favorite. I guess it's an old American custom that a mother dotes on her youngest boy and a father on his eldest. Evelyn wasn't even born yet, so she didn't matter. Not back then.

Dad started taking me on hunting and fishing trips when I was about ten. He said you were too young then, so it was just the two of us. That was when I started calling you "Kid." The name stuck—you liked it—and I still call you that today. I guess Dad and I got used to it being just us, because we kept leaving you home even when you were older; or maybe he wanted it that way, because when I was thirteen, it happened.

He said something like "Men usually have more sex drive than women, but it's an old American custom for men and women to pair up one-on-one. So most men don't get as much sex as they need. We have to learn to pleasure ourselves, or each other." Then he showed me how to masturbate. It was my first actual orgasm, and Kid, it was awesome! But you know about that. You had a first time too.

I was always completely comfortable playing with Dad, so we did it a lot. It wasn't long before he started moving us along. We were cuddled up enjoying that nice afterglow when he raised his hand to my lips and just said "Taste." We moved along pretty fast after that.

Dad explained that I mustn't tell Mom, or you, or anybody at all, for that matter. He said that it's an old American custom that parents can't teach their children about sex. They have to learn it from each other, or in the streets. He said that it's just crazy, and that it guarantees that most kids will get into some kind of trouble, but that it's something we have to live with. He said that violating American customs about sex is worse than murder, or at least that's what people think. We have to do what's right and then be discreet about it. That's how to keep stupid people at bay.

He did say that I should teach what I learned to my buddies, the ones who would have to learn in the streets. He said I could be a good street teacher who balanced out all the bad guys out there. I just had to not say where I learned what I know.

And I did. I found out that my buddies already knew a lot, and we could all learn from each other. We didn't talk about where we learned what we knew. We all knew that was dangerous. I even brought some stuff back to Dad, and pretty soon he and I were doing pretty much everything two men could do together.

We went on that way for several years, and Kid, somehow, we never thought to include you. I guess we both still thought of you as a little kid, and we didn't think about how you were growing up too.

Then everything changed. All of a sudden, war broke out between Mom and Dad; not just quarrelling, hard fighting, like street hoods. We didn't know what was going on, but we did know that we were suddenly cut off and left to take care of ourselves. That's when I realized that you were old enough to teach. That's when I started teaching you. That's when I found out that while Dad had been teaching me, Mom had been teaching you. That's when we both realized what had happened, that Mom was pregnant. That's when we knew that we were all in trouble.

We'd hide in our rooms when they really went at it. At first, we'd just hear things like "So it's okay for you, but not for me? Hello! I don't think so!" Or "No, it's not the same thing at all!" But it got worse, a lot worse, and eventually we'd just leave the house. Sometimes we'd join our buddies down at the old swimming hole and practice some of the stuff Mom and Dad had taught us.

By the time Evelyn was born, the family was in shambles. Friends and neighbors were talking. Some tried to help, but they didn't understand. Apparently, unplanned pregnancies late in life are an old American custom, and apparently, they sometimes wreck families. Nobody thought we were any different. But we were.

When the final big blowup happened, nobody was really surprised. They didn't seriously consider that it was anything more than a marriage gone bad. Everybody knew that Mom had had that postpartum thing, and that they'd even hauled her away once for being a danger to the baby. Everybody knew that Dad was furious about the whole late pregnancy thing, and that he'd started drinking like a fish. It was a simple murder-suicide, maybe even a pact between the two of them. Of course, that's what it was, mostly. There was just a little bit more to it than that.

That little bit more was a big problem. Being older than you, I'd figured out more about American customs than you had. I knew that it was really important that that little bit more stay our secret. Just yours and mine—not even Evelyn can ever know.

I'm gonna marry Lucille Watson, Kid, and we're gonna raise Evelyn just like our own child. I'll tell her the truth, that she's my little sister. I'll never tell her the rest of the truth, that she's also my niece. Not even my wife can ever know that.

I can keep that secret, Kid, but you can't. You think honesty is better. You think the police need to know everything that happened. Of course, if the police know, everybody will know. Everybody will know things about us that could get us lynched. Lynching people is an old American custom, Kid, even here in Rockham.

So, Kid, you have to die. No matter how much I love you, you have to die, and the family secrets have to die with you. I've been thinking about it, thinking hard about it, and I've got some ideas about how to do it and get away with it. I won't let it hurt; at least no more than it has to. I love you, Kid.

I know you talked about having a quiet, simple cremation, but I need a big, public funeral for you. I need an open casket where everybody can see me tuck the envelope with this paper under your white satin pillow. Nobody will think anything of that. It's an old American custom to bury special mementos with your loved ones. Everybody will think I'm doing that, but I won't be. I'll be burying the family secrets with you.

Oh, and by the way, I'll tell them to put you on Mom's side of the plot. Plenty of room for me and mine on Dad's side. And after all, Mom always did like you best.

The Salamander Scripts—
Your Weekly Book Review

In this issue your reviewer looks at *A New Examination of the Salamander Scripts*, a publication by Upstate Press of research toward an advanced degree by Upstate U graduate student Natalie Bumppa. Bumppa's work is significant because for the first time it applies the techniques of modern scholarship to the largely forgotten antique text popularly called *The Salamander Scripts*. Also, it introduces this important historical and anthropological work to a generation that has probably been unaware of it until now.

Bumppa's *New Examination* covers three aspects: (1) the story of the discovery and translation of the *Salamander Scripts*, (2) the story told by the translation itself, and (3) how scholarship has regarded the scripts and how that has changed over time.

For those who do not already know, and this reviewer was among them, *The Salamander Scripts* acquired that (once derogatory) name because they were discovered by maiden sisters Sally and Amanda Scripps upon their inheriting in midlife the crumbling Upstate Winery and Manor House.

While cleaning up the premises and putting the business back into order, Sally noticed peculiar markings on staves of aging barrels being stacked for burning. She ordered those particular staves saved in the cellars, and there but for fate they might have remained to this day. Fate intervened in the form of a Chautauqua production of *Peer Gynt*, where Amanda experienced a *déjà vu* upon sighting runes carved into the walls of the Hall of the Mountain King. Her inquiries led her to meet a handsome set decorator named Sven Arensen, and to invite him to examine the staves.

Arensen declared the staves to be an archaeological treasure bearing authentic runic texts, and he left the Chautauqua troupe at once to attend to their preservation. The sisters gave him room and board at Upstate Manor in exchange for his runic scholarship, and he set about to categorize, sort, and translate the staves. Amanda's training as a stenographer meant that she was admirably suited to be Arensen's assistant, and he grew to depend on her skills.

Alas, Arensen's tenure at Upstate Manor brought not peace, but a sword. Mounting tensions finally erupted into a spectacular arson fire. It utterly destroyed the winery and manor house, it sent Amanda and Sven to meet their maker, and it sent Sally to the Upstate Institute for Wayward Women for the rest of her life. All traces of the original staves were lost, and the only translations that survived were those that Arensen had already shared with critics and potential publishers. These were in various stages of completion, but Arensen had succeeded in sorting the staves chronologically, so that the more complete surviving translations are of the earlier passages.

Bumppa has, for the first time, collected every surviving fragment, so that their story can now be told more completely than ever before.

———•••———

According to Arensen's translation, the first humans of old-world blood in the Americas were twin infants named

Omnibus and Incubus, identical in every way save one—Incubus was black. What disaster stranded them in the new world is unknown, but we do know that they survived by being adopted and suckled by a she-wolf named Delilah.

Delilah followed the seasons and the availability of game up and down the Hudson Valley, so the events recorded in the scripts cover the entire region between Upstate County and the sea. Delilah taught the boys how to den and snuggle for warmth in a place still called Sleepy Hollow. She taught them how to hunt small game for food. She taught them the season for spawning salmon, and at a place still called Fishkill, they learned to capture the fat delicacies swimming upstream. She taught them that rest and relaxation were as important as hunting and fishing, and at a place still called Lake Placid, they spent warm summer days just lying about and napping naked in the sun.

As the boys grew, the trio ranged wider, sometimes reaching as far south as present Virginia. Here the boys learned on their own to supplement their diet of raw meat with various berries, fruits, and nuts. The boys called this "something different." Delilah called it "pica," possibly the first use of the word in this sense in the new world.

Something there is that doesn't love a wolf, and eventually, at a place still called Wolftrap, Delilah met her end. The devastated boys, now old enough to forage for themselves, gave up seasonal migration and settled on the island that Omnibus called *Mannahatta*, because he said that from above it suggested a man with a hat on.

From this point, the translations are only outlines. Omnibus gravitated to the south of the island, where he invented the Battery. Incubus gravitated to the north, where with his son, Apollo, he invented the entertainment industry. Later, both boys developed engineering skills. Omnibus went underground, creating both a transportation system and a successful chain of sandwich shops. Incubus built the bridge after which the father of his country would later be named. And the rest of the story told by the scripts is lost.

————•••————

The discovery and initial translation of *The Salamander Scripts* created some stir in both popular and academic circles of Victorian-era America. Walt Whitman clearly pays homage to the scripts in his poem "Mannahatta," which he calls "the aboriginal name" of his island. (That the resemblance to "a man with a hat on" is not evident to modern observers has been explained in three ways: first, the Harlem River has changed course, second, aerial surveillance was then a primitive technology, or third, hat styles have changed.)

What acceptance the scripts had gained was clearly lost by 1992. The redoubtable *Smithsonian Magazine*, in its Columbian quincentinial article on pre-Columbian claims, dismissed the scripts in one brief paragraph headed "Salamander—Piltdown Man in America."

This reviewer fervently hopes that Natalie Bumppa's new attempts to clarify the history and content of *The Salamander Scripts* will do much to restore their status, especially in scholarly circles. Regrettably, a flagrant publisher's error may work against this. Upstate Press has categorized Bumppa's degree as from the Department of *Creative Writing*. Clearly, this work must have been done towards a degree in history or anthropology. One must urge Upstate Press to correct this grievous error in the next printing, lest this work be ignored by scholarship, and *The Salamander Scripts* be once more lost in the endless cellars of academic archives.

My Five Mothers

First I want to say that it's good to be able to pick my own topic for the first composition of the fifth grade. I don't know if I could stand another "What I Did Last Summer," and anyway, what I really want to talk about is My Five Mothers.

When I ask my father why I have five mothers, he just says that I'm luckier than most boys. If I ask what he means by that he just says that I'll understand it when I get educated. I think that means he's through talking about it.

I don't remember my first mother at all, because she died when I was born. I was just a baby, and it was like I wasn't even there. My father says that I shouldn't feel guilty about her, and I don't know what he means by that. I mean it was like I wasn't even there. Anyway, her name was Helen, and she was pretty and blonde, and I think my father loved her a lot. That's all I really know about her.

My second mother was a French lady. My father always called her Mona something, which was pretty silly if you ask me, since her real name was Jacqueline des Jardins. I know that because she taught me how to spell it.

Anyway, I liked Mona. She taught me how things ought to have names. She had a big shoulder purse named Coco and a Japanese fan named Fran. She took me to kindergarten in a yellow RX8 named Ahura Mazda, after somebody who got famous for being good. My father didn't like that, for some reason. He said, "Ahura Mazda is a Persian god. You think your car is a god?" Mona said he was inscrutable, and she and I named his big old Chevy Vlad the Impala, after somebody who got famous for being bad. She said it's what people used to call Dracula. We named my old one-piece pajamas Mickey, because they were covered with Mickey Mouse pictures.

Mona was the kind of mother who is always baking stuff, like cakes and brownies and breads. My father called her a master baker, and he said we needed to pronounce that carefully. I asked why, and he said I'd understand it when I got educated.

For my breakfast Mona used to feed me jam and a kind of French bread she made called a croissant. I remember, because when I couldn't remember that name, my father told me to think of my old maid Aunt Edna. Now it's true that Aunt Edna is a cross aunt—she always seems cross about something. When I asked my father why that was, he said that he wasn't sure, but it could be because she never really got educated. Mona thought that was so funny she choked on her jam, and they both giggled on and off until breakfast was over. Maybe that was when I first started realizing that when my father talks about getting educated, he means more than just going to school.

Another thing that was nice about the Mona days was that Uncle Bert always used to come to visit. I liked Uncle Bert, and he would always bring me some special toy or game or something "to keep him busy." But one day I came home from kindergarten and found Mona crying and packing Coco and all her other stuff into Ahura Mazda. She drove away and never came back, and neither did Uncle Bert. I asked my father what had happened, and he said that I'd have to wait until I was educated to understand it.

Not long after Mona left, my third and fourth mothers came. They were twins named Cora and Dora Wallis. I couldn't tell them apart, so I just called each one Ora. They didn't like it at first, but they got used to it. I asked my father how he told them apart, and he said that they had different tattoos. I couldn't see that, and he said of course not, and that I'd understand it when I got educated.

The Oras were thin and fidgety, with short black hair and dark tans. They were always running around to yoga classes and meditation groups and stuff. They drove me to and from school in twin pink Mustangs that didn't have names, so I decided to name them. One day at dinner I announced that I'd named them Hor-ass and Mor-ass, saying them both so they'd rhyme, and that they ought to have license plates saying that. Everybody stopped chewing and just stared at me with their mouths open. My father even had green pea soup dripping from one side of his mouth. Finally, my father said "Oh, *Horace* and *Morris!*" and everybody laughed and started chewing again. I asked what was going on, and my father said that I'd said it funny, and that they thought I'd meant something else, and that I'd understand when I got educated. Everybody giggled off and on until dinner was over.

The Oras fed me cold cereal for breakfast. I didn't like that, and my father said that I should at least have an egg, because I was a growing boy and growing boys ought to be able to tell that they'd been fed. I could tell I was a growing boy, because I always needed bigger clothes. My new pajamas had Star Wars pictures all over them, so I named them Chewbacca. Anyway, eventually I got an egg too.

A nice thing about the Oras was that since there were two of them, they had more time to do stuff with me. But they still spent most of their time with my father. One time one of them asked my father what time the man from the ad was coming, and that's how I first met Raul.

For a little while, Raul and the Oras and my father spent a lot of time together, but then one day my father picked me up from school in Vlad instead of one of the Oras in one of the Mustangs. When we got home the Oras were gone, but Raul was still there. And that's how I got my fifth mother.

Raul is a really neat guy. He's got black hair and a beard and mustache, and he talks with some kind of accent. He keeps a set of barbells down in the basement, and he's always playing with them, so he's got a lot of muscles. He knows it's important to name things. Like he calls his cup of tea Earl Grey. He told me I should start calling my father Dad, and I tried it and it works! I asked Raul if I should call him Mom, but he said no, that Raul was fine.

Raul takes me to school in a red Corvette convertible named Thrust, which everybody thinks is just too cool. Oh, I know Katy's mother brings her in a Corvette, but it's just plain white, and it has a top, and I bet it doesn't even have a name. Besides, Katy's mother always wears a shirt.

Raul feeds me Spanish omelets for breakfast, and when you've had one of Raul's Spanish omelets you know you've been fed. That's important for a growing boy—Dad said so. And when Raul bought me new pajamas, he said I should just get plaid, because I've outgrown all that cartoon stuff. He told me that plaid was from Scotland, and we named my plaid pajamas Charlie, after a Bonnie Prince Charlie, who used to be from Scotland.

I told Dad that I really liked Raul and that I hoped he'd be my mother for a long time. Dad said that he probably would, because he thought he knew now what had been wrong with his other relationships. I asked him what he meant, and he said that I'd understand it when I got educated, and that I'd probably get educated faster with Raul in the house. Raul choked on Earl Grey when he heard that, but I don't think it was because it was funny. Dad said that he didn't mean it *that* way, and Raul got okay again, and they both laughed about it. I guess I'll understand that when I get educated, too.

Raul can do things none of my other mothers could do. He can throw a fast ball that stings my hand right through Casey, my catcher's mitt. He can pick me up and swing me into Thrust without even opening the door, and I've never seen anybody else's mother do that. He takes me to neat places like Zachary, the zoo, and Aaron, the airplane museum.

So, I guess when Dad says that I'm lucky to have five mothers he's right. But mostly I'm lucky to have Raul. I mean this is not just like having five mothers; it's like having two fathers. Oh, I know Minnie has two fathers, but they live in separate towns and don't speak to each other, and what good is that?

Raul told Dad that when school is out, we must all three go somewhere interesting and do something fun for the summer. He talks about a family nudist resort in Florida, and that sounds like fun. I've never seen Florida. So, I'm hoping that if in the sixth grade I have to write about "What I Did Last Summer," I'll have some neat stuff to write about.

And in the meantime, I'm already making progress on getting educated. Like when Raul bought me those new pajamas, I overheard dad say, "He'll sleep naked when he gets educated." Dad has always slept naked, and I guess he's educated, so now I do too. Besides, that sounds like a good way to get ready for that resort in Florida. Do you think it counts?

The Ballad of Canbia and Polly Ann

I feel so, so *used*," Polly Ann sobbed. "And I feel so, so *stupid*! How could I have been so, so *naïve*?" I fumbled around in my pockets and found a clean handkerchief. Lucky, I guess; I always carry a handkerchief, but never a clean one. Allergies, you know.

"He was nothing but a con man all the time! He conned *everybody*! Not just me! He conned everybody in Canbia, and he conned the editor of the *Eagle*! The very *editor*! How can you *do* that? How can *anybody* do that?"

"He," of course, was Yossef Yutu, Polly Ann's erstwhile husband, whom I gathered had just up and disappeared. My handkerchief was getting kinda wet, so I looked around for some tissues. Polly Ann's kitchen was a disaster, but I found a roll of paper towels. Good thing too. She was running like Niagara.

"He was bizarre," Polly Ann said when she was finally a little more composed. "Bizarre. There isn't any other word for him. He was everything to everybody, and the bizarre thing was that he never seemed a contradiction. When I saw him as the gentle patron of all those little old ladies from the old country, and then as the hard-nosed adversary of that public park in the Canbia district, I should have thought he was a two-faced scoundrel. But I didn't. Nobody did. It was like he had us all hypnotized, and we could only see the good in him. "Now I've got no job; I've got no husband; I've got no reputation; I've got *nothing*! Nothing at all! What am I gonna *do*, Teddy? What am I gonna *do*?"

I was more worried about what *I* was going to do. I had a life out there, and a job that I was supposed to be doing. But I also had an old friend in trouble; a pal from way back whom I couldn't just leave alone in a crisis. Polly Ann and I had been buddies since grade school, when she'd played first base with the boys during morning recess. We'd dated in high school, but it was never anything romantic; we were just best buddies and it was handy to have a steady date. But we went to different colleges, and we almost lost touch. She knew from the get-go that she wanted to be a reporter for *The Wichita Eagle*, and after graduation she went straight there and got an entry-level job.

I wanted to be a rock god, but I got over it. Then I tried astrophysics, but I got over that too. By the time I tried newspaper work, Polly Ann already had a good spot at the *Eagle* and had a clear career path ahead of her. I got a job as a cub reporter, and she was my boss. It didn't take long for us to become best buds all over again.

But then in 1989, she met Yossef and everything changed.

———•••———

I remember a conversation shortly after that fateful meeting. Polly Ann was almost apologetic. "I can't explain it, Teddy. He's not handsome or rich or witty or hung. He's not anything I've ever thought I'd want in a man. He's short and scruffy, and he has a heavy accent, Ukrainian or something, and he dresses like he just got off the boat from somewhere really far off. But I really just like being around him and talking with him. He knows a lot about almost everything, but he knows how to make me think I'm telling him things he never knew. And when I introduce him to somebody, he knows just what to say to get them talking about themselves, and to make them think he's really interested in them. And when he meets them again, even weeks later, he remembers every little thing they said the last time and he picks right up where they left off. Oh, I suppose I should just think he's read Dale Carnegie and knows "how to win friends and influence people," but it all comes to him so naturally that I can't believe it's something he's learned."

Polly Ann was swept off her feet, and not long after that conversation, she actually married Yossef.

———••———

Last year, when Yossef decided to run for Wichita City Council as the councilman from the Canbia district, I got the assignment of raking up everything I could find on him, for *The Wichita Eagle*. The paper needed to know whether to endorse the man or expose him as some kind of fraud, and I was the designated dirt digger. I dug here and I dug there, and I became more and more confused.

I learned that when Yossef first appeared in Wichita from some unnamed place in eastern Europe, he gravitated at once to Canbia, a section often called The Ghetto. He befriended all those "little old ladies from the old country," as Polly Ann put it, at once. It sounded as if those old ladies knew Yossef better than anybody else, and since, if he won a council seat, these would be his constituents, I started there, with Polly Ann's neighbor Sonia Krumholtz. I found that she *adored* Yossef.

"Just to be around Yossef was to bring back memories of being a little girl back in the old country," Mrs. Krumholtz remembered. "He reminded me so much of my old *rebbe*. Oh, Yossef was not old, no, not old, but he understood things that you think only an old man would understand, you know? An old man has seen so much trouble and so much happiness, and an old man can see your trouble and your happiness without asking, you know? My old Rebbe was like that, and Yossef was like that, like an old rebbe who can see all the things you try to hide, and who understands you without asking. I always felt so peaceful with my old rebbe, because there was no reason to pretend anything. No reason." She daubed her old eyes with a dark silk kerchief. "And Yossef was like that. With Yossef there was no reason to pretend. No reason to hide. With Yossef everything was peaceful and right.

"When my Benny was born, my great-grandson Benjamin, I wanted Yossef to be the *mohel* at his *bris*—you know about the *bris*? I wanted Yossef, but he reminded me that he was not my rebbe, and he should not be the one. I was surprised, because I forgot that Yossef was a *goy*. I am an old woman, and I forget. I forget, or maybe I remember. I remember my old rebbe, and I remember being a girl back in the old country, you know? I am an old woman and I remember."

Mrs. Krumholtz didn't really give me much to go on, so I moved on to Police Chief Rocky Shore. If Yossef had a record, surely the chief would know.

"No," the chief said, "Yossef is clean so far as we know. I admit I was a little leery of him at first, when he arrived here from someplace in eastern Europe, I forget just where. I did check with Interpol, and he wasn't on their books anywhere. I decided he was just kinda different from your average Kansas fellow, but still pretty harmless.

"And it didn't take Yossef long to become a fixture in Cambia. He has a knack for making friends, and he knows how to stand out in any crowd. I guess I'd call him *charismatic*, but not in the bad way some people use that word. I think he's a good man who really has the community's interest at heart, and we ought to cultivate him and use him for the common good. I've encouraged him to get involved with the community, maybe even the local government.

"Of course, he does have his idiosyncrasies. He still dresses and grooms like an old-world man, and that turns some people off. And he's a regular nut for Steven Sondheim, particularly *Gypsy*, and particularly the line 'Wichita's one and only burlesque theater presents Miss Gypsy Rose Lee!' It just ties his passion for Sondheim to his passion for Wichita, so it's probably harmless. But it's still a little crazy, especially since everybody around here knows that Gypsy Rose Lee first performed in Kansas City, not Wichita at all."

The chief's opinion of Yossef wasn't exactly a ringing endorsement, but I didn't see any reason Yossef couldn't make a good councilman. I wanted more, so I talked with Randy Tarr, editor of the *Star*, Yossef's little newspaper. He had definite opinions about Yossef, and he shared them freely.

"Why Yossef would want a newspaper, I didn't know. Wichita didn't need another newspaper; the *Eagle* is everywhere, and everybody reads it. But Youssef said that Canbia could use its own little neighborhood rag, one of those throw-aways, you know, free to the public and supported by ads. Canbia is just a little corner of Wichita, but it's got its own unique flavor, and its own special style, and if there were a rag that catered just to that flavor and style, well, people would read it. And if people would read it, then merchants would buy ads in it. Local merchants trying to reach local people. Yossef said that the *Eagle* was too big for that, and he said there was a need.

"And Yossef wanted to call his newspaper the *Star*. I told him that name had been sullied, and it made people think of big-eyed aliens and two-headed babies and stuff like that. But he knew better—Yossef always knew better, and a lot of the time he was right—so I shut up."

Yossef was beginning to sound like a two-headed baby himself. I moved on to retiring City Councilman Walker Totterman, the man Yossef had hoped to succeed.

"When Yossef approached me about running for City Council, I thought he must be joking. Yes, I was going to retire, and no, I hadn't anointed any successor, but I'd thought somebody would pop up. Somebody from the political establishment, I mean. Yossef was a nobody, an amateur, a total stranger to Wichita politics. But I have to admit that I was impressed by the man, after spending some time and talking about things. He had a remarkable grasp of Canbia politics, Wichita politics, even. He understood Wichita's position in state and national affairs, and he had good ideas about what was wrong and what might be done to fix it. I couldn't endorse him, after just one meeting, but I decided not to stand in his way. Canbia could do a lot worse!"

<hr />

But all those interviews were from last year. Yossef had already wooed and won Polly Ann, and she had already married him. He had already wooed her away from the *Eagle* and set her up as managing editor of the *Star*. But a lot more had happened since then. Yossef did run for city councilman, and he plotted with Polly Ann how to market his name. He reminded her of his idol Sondheim, "Steven says you need to get a gimmick if you want to be a star."

"Okay, *Schatzi*" he said. "I want you to canvass all the *Star*'s readers. Ask them what I can do to get this face imprinted on every mind in Canbia. I need a gimmick. Not a political gimmick, mind you. My positions on the issues are clear. I need a way to get noticed. And if you make it a contest, my little *Schatz*, if you make people compete to find a way to make me noticeable, then that *will be* the gimmick! Everybody in Canbia will have already noticed me, and we won't even need their contest entries. Get it? Write an article for the *Star* and maybe we can even get it reprinted in the *Eagle*." Polly Ann thought it was a cute idea, and she wrote and printed the article. And yes, the *Eagle* promised to pick it up.

But then everything seemed to have gone seriously awry. Yossef had skipped town leaving everybody and everything in the lurch. Right now, I needed to comfort Polly Ann, but first I needed to understand more. It was time to find out what the hell was going on *now*. First I went back to Police Chief Rocky Shore. He had plenty to tell!

———————

"First, his name's not Yossef Yutu, it's Anatol Rief, or at least we think it is. He's a sort of international *Till Eulenspiegel*, who lives to play complicated practical jokes on people, or even on cities or countries. He spends years setting up a caper, then springs his trap while he hops a jet plane to the other side of the earth and disappears. He must have billions stashed away somewhere, because he does all this stuff and never needs money. He's wanted all over the world. Today, we've managed to trace him to a one-way ticket to New York, with connection to Paris and then on to God knows where."

Just then a sergeant burst into the room. "Chief, we've traced him to Minsk, but that's the end of it. Nothing more to go on. Nobody in Minsk is gonna help us, at least not without a specific charge against him. Apparently that's one of the few places in Europe where he's *not* wanted. Looks like we've hit a brick wall."

The chief sighed. "You'll remember I called him *charismatic*. Well, today maybe I'd even say *messianic*, and I'd say such men are dangerous. But back then, he managed to disarm even me. Okay, I was naïve. I was just as vulnerable as anybody else in Cambia. But I've learned, and nothing like this is going to happen in Wichita again, at least not on my watch. I didn't think I had anything left to learn, but now I've learned that that was a really wrong-headed notion. I've learned that, and I've set out to learn more every day from now on. Nobody is too smart to learn more, not even me. It's kind of like the heavens opened for me, you know? Everything is different now. And everything is going to be better now. I guess we can thank Yossef for that."

Yossef was getting more interesting every moment. I hurried back to Randy Tarr at the *Star*.

"What a damn mess!" Randy said. "On the other hand, what a well-tied-up mess. Yossef, or Anatol, or whoever he is, just blew up everything he was involved in, and then in the last second, tied everything up in nice little bows and left everything easy to pick up. The man is a madman. The man is a genius. The man is impossible. The man is my hero!"

I interrupted. "Hold on now. Just tell me what happened. What's gonna happen to the *Star*, and to Polly Ann's job? And what about her marriage?"

Randy beamed with pride. "I own the *Star*, lock, stock and barrel, and it's got enough money in the bank to run for another year whether we sell any ads or not. Polly Ann is editor-in-chief, with a better salary than she ever got at the *Eagle*. We're both sitting pretty, as they say. As to the marriage, it's annulled, all right and proper, and Polly Ann has a small fortune in the bank. When she gets over the shock, she's gonna be one glad, glad girl."

Curiouser and curiouser!

I hurried back to Polly Ann's place to see how much of this she'd actually processed. I found a much calmer woman—in fact, a slightly inebriated one—taking tea with Sonia Krumholtz, and tipsily singing one of Yossef's favorite songs from *Gypsy*: "So get yourself a gimmick, and you, too, can be a star." She saw me and broke off singing.

"Oh, Teddy, I'm *soo* glad you came! Everything is *soo* much better now. I understand Yossef for the very first time, and I love him, I *just love him*, Teddy! He's left me *rich* and *employed* and the very *talk* of Wichita. And that's in a good way, Teddy. A good way. And now I understand why he made me stop using my whole name. He wouldn't let me write for the *Star* as Polly Ann, you know. It had to be just Ann. But now it's all over and I can go back to being Polly Ann, and I'm *just so happy*, Teddy!"

Mrs. Krumholtz broke in. "Where are her manners, I ask you! Sit down and take some tea. And you must try my special linzertorte. It's my grandmama's recipe from the old country and it wins prizes. Yes, it wins prizes everywhere. My old rebbe used to come by our house every Friday just to be there when it came out of the oven." She was dishing up the most decadent pastry I'd ever seen, with a lattice top over a layer of red jam over God knows what else, but I could smell hazelnuts and almonds. "Here, eat," she commanded.

Polly Ann dished up another helping for herself. The red jam on her lips testified that she'd already been pigging out. She took a big forkful and continued her story. "The *Eagle* reprinted the piece I'd run in the *Star*," she bubbled. "And it turned out just as Yossef planned. He set all this up just so the *Eagle* would run this piece. Then his joke was sprung, and his work was done, and he just slipped away. But first he tied up all the loose ends, and left everything all proper and everybody all happy, I just love him, Teddy. I just love him."

"Hold it right there," I interrupted. Just what did Yossef do? What was this work that was all done?"

"Oh, didn't I say?" She handed me the Sunday *Eagle's* op-ed page. "Here, see for yourself."

And then it all came clear. Yossef was rich enough and mad enough to invest years of his life just to produce this little one-line pun and to get it published for the world to see. What a mad genius! What attention to detail it must have taken!

I read the caption and the byline. Polly Ann was grinning at me as she hummed bits of Sondheim's tune. I looked at the paper again and read: "Get Yossef a Gimmick—Ann Yutu, *Canbia Star*."

The Archangel's Trumpet

Santa Juanita was a sleepy Mexican town in all ways but one—it was the seat of a bishop, so it could rightly call its small but fortresslike church a cathedral. The bishop's realm included most of Mexico's northern frontier lands, some still uncharted. Mexico City was far away, and so was any other real government, so Bishop Antonio Aquinas was the only authority of any consequence for hundreds of miles around. This authority he wielded in the style of a benevolent despot.

When garbed in his vestments of office the bishop was a formidable sight, one that the ignorant might easily mistake for the Lord God himself, and might believe him able to direct the mighty thunderbolts that sometimes walked the local mountains in summertime. His reputation was for sternness, but for fairness toward widows and orphans and other downtrodden. For landowners and highwaymen, he gave as much justice as their money could buy. The bishop also sold indulgences freely, so his purse and those of the cathedral and the attached abbey grew heavy with time.

Times changed, wars were fought, treaties were signed, and borders were adjusted. One day Bishop Aquinas awoke to find that his town and his cathedral were now under the jurisdiction of the United States of America. At once, the trickle of English-speaking travelers from the East grew into a steady stream, among them soldiers and government officials. The bishop realized that his days of supreme authority could be numbered. As his anxieties grew, his work began to suffer.

So it was that, when one of the travelers turned out to be a Chicago soothsayer of some repute, the bishop saw an opportunity to put his mind at ease. His English being fairly good, he visited the wise man, and for a sum calculated to elicit a favorable response, asked him to predict just how long his power was destined to last.

The soothsayer performed certain rituals and delivered his answer. "Bishop Aquinas shall not fall," he pronounced, "'til the archangel's trumpet blows in the nave. I regret that I cannot be more precise, but that is all that I sense."

No matter. The bishop knew exactly what the omen meant, he knew exactly what he must do, and he knew that he must do it before Easter. He called Brother Iago, the most trusted of his monks, and together they took a torch into the dimness of the church. High above them in the nave an eclectic mix of saints and apostles, angels and demons, and ritual objects of all sorts decorated the walls and ceiling. The bishop waved his torch about and spotted what he was looking for. An effigy of the Archangel Gabriel raised a slender herald's trumpet from his lips to the heavens.

"Iago," he asked, "am I right that that is a real trumpet and not just a dummy?"

"Oh yes, Your Grace," Iago answered. "That is the one we use every year for Easter services, so it is in good repair. Shall I get it down and play it for you?"

"Absolutely not!" cried the bishop. "My wish is that it should never play again. Get it down, but punch holes in its backside and fill it with adobe. When you are sure that it can never sound again put it back up there. While you have it down, be certain that neither you nor anyone else blows it."

Brother Iago was taken aback, but being used to absolute obedience to his bishop, he made no protest. He followed his orders, and when the ruined trumpet was once again in

Gabriel's hands, he reported back to his master. The bishop rewarded him handsomely with a magnificent package of indulgences, including those little vices that are so precious to a cloistered monk. Relieved of his anxieties, Bishop Aquinas threw himself back into his work with renewed vigor. Once again, he dispatched justice from the cathedral, with sternness and with the traditional sort of fairness.

Easter came and went, the rising sun being summoned successfully, in the absence of the trumpet, by a quartet of guitars. Ministers from the United States capital came to request the bishop's cooperation in setting up new local government structures, but they were turned away without an audience. Eventually, United States soldiers set up an encampment near the cathedral, but Bishop Aquinas paid them no mind. Prophecy had assured him that they could do him no harm.

The day came when the abbot brought a slender, wan youth before the bishop and accused him of most grievous crimes. "This boy," the accuser claimed, "has been corrupting the bodies and minds of your monks for weeks. He commits unspeakable acts with them, sometimes right in the cathedral itself! No punishment would be too extreme for him."

Righteous indignation flamed within the bishop's heart, if only because he knew that this lad had not bought the necessary indulgences. Still, he was determined to follow just procedure. "Who are you," he demanded, "Where do you come from? Why are you here?"

"I am Igor Romanov," the fey youth declared. "I live by selling my favors, and your monks have been very good to me. I was born in the city of Archangel, in Russia, but I come here by way of San Francisco, where," and he swelled with pride, "they call me The Strumpet—The Archangel Strumpet."

Bishop Aquinas blanched; he choked; he fainted dead away. At that moment, a great shout arose from the courtyard. American forces had entered the cathedral grounds, and the rule of the Bishop of Santa Juanita was at an end.

And the Archangel Strumpet? He simply walked away, a free man.

The Momentous Occasions of Professor Ted Miller

Cora Caballo steered Ted Miller down an endless hallway that hummed dangerously of rushing air and straining transformers, and that smelled faintly of ozone and fear. The plain sheetrock walls were broken by endless identical doors and an occasional intersection with another featureless hallway. The entire scene was lit by a long string of tired fluorescent tubes in various states of yellow decay.

This was the physics building at Gower U, but there were no students rushing from class to class. This was the sub-basement, where all the secret research labs hid from prying undergraduate eyes. Universities are wont to contract their services to private companies and government organizations that are involved in shady (through student eyes) activities. Students are wont to protest such involvements, so it is best to simply keep them out of sight.

The sterile place contrasted sharply with the old couple, academically dressed in suede-elbow tweeds. "This must be what it's like in a submarine," Cora said. "It's great that Mark has a birthday surprise for you, but why must we meet him in his lab?" She strode purposefully from door to numbered door, comparing each with a slip of paper, through the bottoms of trifocals.

Ted stumbled to keep up, his thin old legs working to stay coordinated. "I'd call it the Labyrinth! I keep expecting a minotaur!" He peered down a cross hall through the tops of trifocals, running nervous fingers through thin white hair. "I do hope this 'surprise' is not some laboratory concoction of Purple Jesus Punch."

"Not Likely. Mark is physics. That would be chemistry. Or fraternity." Cora laughed at her little joke.

She was what people call a "horsey woman," with big features and a strong voice. "Oh, this is it," she neighed, knocking on a numbered door.

The door burst open with an explosion of bright blue-white light, revealing a jet-black beard and a threadbare lab coat. "Welcome, welcome!" cried Mark Allison, "Welcome to the most secret lab at Gower U. Come right in and have a look around!" Mark was tall and dark, fortyish, with the serious mien of the workaholic.

Cora blinked her eyes and took in the room. Keyboards and display screens were everywhere, with systems of pipes and networks of multicolored cables and black boxes bristling with knobs and indicator lights. There were no windows or any other nod to the existence of an outside world. "Yep, a submarine," she said. "Nuclear, from the look of it. And is this awful light Cherenkov radiation?"

Ted looked puzzled. "Cherenkov radiation?"

Cora turned pedantic. "Cherenkov radiation is light produced when something moves faster than the speed of light, a paradox that physicists are able to explain away somehow. The Cherenkov radiation from a nuclear reactor is blue."

"Ah," Mark exclaimed. "The little lady from English Lit. has done her homework before coming to the evil physics lab! I'm impressed!"

Cora peered accusingly at Mark over her glasses. "Don't be. Everybody reads the papers. Well, almost everybody."

Mark ignored the slight. "Today you will see things that

nobody else has seen; at least not yet. You see, when you have both tenure *and* an independent income, you can do pretty much what you want, and you don't have to explain yourself to anybody until you're good and ready. Well, I've got both, and I've been working on the nature of *time*. I've finally got something really earthshaking to announce to the world. But not yet; first, I'm going to show it to *you*."

"Not another cold fusion, I hope." Cora challenged. "We've had enough of that." She looked condescendingly at Ted's expression, puzzled again, and explained. "You remember how back in '89 Fleischman and Pons claimed to have done nuclear fusion on a table top, at room temperature. That was at least wrong, and probably a hoax."

"*Time*, Cora, *Time*. Not nuclear." Mark sighed. "Apparently, a little homework is a dangerous thing. Now pay attention.

"Believe it or not, we can now observe events that happened in the past! I figured it out after I learned about memory mapping in computers. We can do time mapping the same way. We just have to map an interval of *here and now* onto an interval of *then and there*. It took me a while to figure out how to do that, but now I have.

"Now Ted, I understand that today marks two momentous occasions in your life. You turn seventy-five, and you retire from the History Department and take on that honorable title of professor emeritus."

"Ah, yes," Ted smiled. "They say it's from the Latin *ex*, meaning 'out of,' and *meritus*, meaning 'earned."

"Wonderful," neighed Cora, "So you are just where you ought to be at this moment. That's a measure of success, isn't it?"

Mark ignored her again and led the way into an inner room. "Dr. Miller, on these two momentous occasions in your life, we are going to visit your very first momentous occasion, at that St. Louis trolley stop where you were born."

"Wouldn't it be more sensible to visit tomorrow's lottery drawing?" Cora asked. Cora was not only a horsey woman, but a practical one.

"Well, that *would* have certain advantages," Mark agreed, "but unfortunately we can't go to anywhere that hasn't happened yet; at least not yet. And you'll enjoy the St. Louis visit. We've all heard the story and had lots of good laughs about it, but imagine seeing it firsthand! Besides, Cora's dressed for it, or did you just come from the Derby?"

Cora sniffed. "Mother said I'd never go wrong with houndstooth and spectator pumps."

"Well, when it's *your* birthday, we'll visit a time where Mother was right," Mark replied. "But not yet; today is Ted's day."

"It *would* be rather droll to actually see what happened," Ted mused. "Poor Momma talked about it so much, and I've always wondered if the tale grew in the telling. She even claimed that there were shots fired, and that just had to be her imagination."

"What I can't imagine is how there can have been nobody at all there to help her," Mark said.

"There was an awful heat wave," Ted explained. "It was a miserable day, and only mad dogs and Englishmen were out and about. There *were* several tourists at the trolley stop, but they spoke no English, and they were no help at all. The afterbirth came in the trolley car. Can you imagine the mess?"

"Well," Cora said decisively, "I'm not going *anywhere* in an untested gadget built by a mad scientist. Sorry, make that *anywhen*."

"Cora, you're in a physics lab. 'When' and 'where' are the same thing. And besides, it's not a 'gadget,' and it's not untested." Mark wheeled out a cage with a small alert monkey. "Meet Mikey and see some of the pictures he helped take." He spread out half a dozen brightly colored photographs on the table.

"Mark, those are photos of the Hindenburg disaster!" Ted gasped. "In full color and from the air! How did you...?"

"I sent Mikey and his cage back for just a minute, and the camera snapped what he looked at. Aren't they fantastic? Look at the color! Hydrogen burns blue, and there it is!" The popular notion that the Hindenburg went down in an encompassing ball of bright red and yellow fire is simply wrong. It was a dim blue flame that the black-and-white film of the day was especially sensitive to. The lighter-than-air hydrogen burned as it escaped upward from the airship. There was no fire in the passenger gondola at all, but of course there was hot metal falling all around.

Ted and Cora stared dumbly, first at the photos, then at Mark, then at Mikey.

"And in this one, see that man, way down there, with the microphone? That's Herb Morrison, the reporter. Remember?"

"'Oh, the humanity!'" Cora quoted. "That changed news reporting forever!" She responded to Ted's puzzlement before he could ask. "Morrison's coverage of that Zeppelin's arrival was an early try at real-time reporting. He's infamous now for completely losing his cool when the thing blew up."

"And compare the camera angle with this original. See that little smudge that people think is equipment being blown away?"

"My God!" Ted cried. "Are you telling me...?"

"Yes! It's Mikey's monkey cage! So you see, he was there, so he *had to* go back! And he was just fine when he got back here. A little confused, but that's to be expected. After all, he'd just seen a perfectly ordinary airship explode into a major fireball. Well, maybe he *was* a little singed, but then you can see he *was* at close range.

"Now I've already mapped the precise coordinates of the beginning and end of our visit, both here and there. We'll be there for just a few minutes, but it'll be enough. We don't need to get into any machine or anything. Just stand in a circle right here." Mark knew that he mustn't give anyone a chance for more second thoughts. He pressed a button on a hand-held remote.

There was a deafening roar and the world went white.

———•••———

Then they were stumbling onto a wretchedly hot, humid street corner in an old-fashioned neighborhood. Ted was opening and closing his mouth like a fish out of water and whimpering like a puppy on his first night alone. Mark was yelling "My leg! I'm bleeding! Help me!" Cora was giggling crazily, but she pulled herself together and looked around her.

A loud, garbled voice from behind them called her attention to a uniformed policeman, shouting into the mouthpiece of an old-fashioned police call box. The air filled with loud mechanical noise. "Here comes the trolley," Cora cried as a ramshackle electric car lumbered noisily around a curve. The car rattled up to them and jerked to a stop.

"The driver's getting out!" Cora exclaimed. "Why is he backing down? Oh, I see—somebody's handing him something from inside."

The driver backed down the steps and whirled around with a snarl. He angrily stuffed something into Ted's unwilling arms—a naked, bloody, screaming infant, its knotted umbilical cord still dangling.

"Uh, what's this?" Ted croaked stupidly.

The driver glared but didn't answer. Still snarling, he motioned to the policeman. Both leaped back into the car, and when they emerged a moment later, each held one arm of a half-conscious woman. They lowered her, half walking, half sliding, down the steps.

"What are you doing?" Mark and Cora yelled in unison, but the men ignored them and dragged the woman to a streetlamp post, where they dropped her into a wet, bloody puddle. Ted just stared open-mouthed at the screaming baby and made little whimpering sounds.

The policeman yipped like a coyote and jumped out of the group, and the driver, still snarling, tore the baby away from Ted. Grabbing it by the feet and swinging it in the air, he gave it a sharp slap on the back. The baby went silent and limp, but the driver gave it two more sharp slaps anyway. "He's killed it!" Cora screamed.

The prone woman spread her legs and the driver discarded the little body on the ground between them. Dropping to his knees and still snarling, the driver produced a pocket knife and somehow used it to reattach the umbilical cord. Then he undid the knot in the cord.

Everybody screamed as the little legs inserted themselves into the woman's body. The woman writhed and shrieked and sucked the whole baby inside. When only its little bald pate was still visible, the driver, finding fragments of cotton underwear wrapped about the woman's thighs, pulled them together to make a complete undergarment. Somehow, he used the pocket knife to fuse the parts together. Then he snarled some more, pocketed the knife, and jumped back into the car, which sped away with a loud screeching of brakes.

The woman pulled her legs together and moaned. She grabbed the lamp post with frantic hands, and Mark and Ted both jumped to grab her hands and help, though they had no notion of how. At that instant, a bullet zinged through Mark's leg, healing it completely, and stopping all blood flow. Several more bullets flew by but failed to hit anything. Distant yelling revealed the policeman, now a block away, waving a gun and disappearing around a corner.

"He thinks you're attacking her!" Cora shouted. "Back off!"

But the men couldn't back off; they were glued to the woman. She ascended the lamppost like a hoisted flag, screaming all the time. The men hung onto her arms until she was upright, then let go and sprang back. "Garbledy *eep!*" Screeched the woman. "Garbledy *eep!*"

"We're the tourists!" Mark shouted.

"But we speak English!" Cora cried.

"Not *that* English," Mark pointed to the still babbling woman. "Nobody speaks that English. We're the tourists— *we were there*—so we *had to* go back! Don't you see?"

The woman, drenched and disheveled, but now a bit more composed, turned and stared after the retreating trolley. Suddenly things seemed almost in control.

"Mark, you idiot, you mapped those coordinates *backwards*," Ted accused.

But Mark was ecstatic. "It's unbelievable! We've touched on one of the greatest mysteries of modern science, *the arrow of time: why does consciousness experience time only as a one-directional flow?* Nobody knows the answer; at least not yet! Have I got my work cut out for me when we get back!"

"Well, now we know why Mikey was a little confused," Cora said. "He'd just seen a major fireball reintegrate itself into a perfectly ordinary airship. I'm surprised he didn't mention it."

The men stared at Cora for only a moment, and then they all broke out laughing.

"Still, I don't get it," she continued. Everything around us is going backward, but we're not talking backward. What's going on? Will I be younger when we get back?"

"*Younger!*" Ted exclaimed. "I'm going to be ten years *older*! Nobody should be doing this sort of thing at my time of life!"

"Maybe we *are* talking backward," Mark ventured. "Maybe we're hearing backward too, and it cancels out. But they're talking forward, and we're hearing it backward. It's crazy! It's wonderful! Some things are following our time, and some theirs! Nobody has ever seen anything like this, at least not yet!"

Ted was suddenly serious. "Mark, that bullet wound—that went backwards, for us; all that blood flowed *into* your leg. But there must be something like a law of conservation of cause and effect. What's going to happen when we get back? Remember, Mikey *was* a little singed."

Mark sobered. "I see what you mean. Normally, things that were different when we left here would still be different when we got back. But now, it's things that were different when we *got* here that will be different when we get back. I could be in real trouble. Well, we'll find out pretty soon." He looked at his watch. "This is about when we were supposed to arrive. Everybody stand in a circle, now."

Then there was a deafening roar and the world went white.

———✦••✦———

And they were all stumbling onto Mark's laboratory floor. Cora was giggling crazily. Ted was opening and closing his mouth like a fish out of water and whimpering like a puppy on his first night alone. Mark was yelling "My leg! I'm bleeding! Help me!"

Mark Allison did not further develop his work on the nature of time. His femoral artery was severed, and he bled out there on his laboratory floor. His successor at Gower University dismantled the lab after despairing of what it might be good for. He dismissed the Hindenburg photos as ordinary virtual reality printouts. He hasn't a clue; at least not yet.

Ted Miller now does his guppy and puppy imitations in a small, picturesque sanatorium in Simi Valley. His final "momentous occasion" has not come; not yet.

Cora Caballo took orders in a Buddhist convent in the Himalayas. She sees no one; at least not yet.

Mikey the monkey was sent to the Yerkes Sanctuary for Retired Laboratory Primates, and from there was adopted by one Maryanne Moegelsturm. Maryanne herself is actually a great grandniece of Herb Morrison, but neither she nor Mikey know about that special bond between them.

At least, not yet.

Escape from Persepolis

B ogey at 2 o'clock, 2 high!" Captain Roper cried, alarm in her voice. "Security, scan him and report."

Roper was head controller at the Pearl Harbor Geostationary space hub, Pearl Geo. Her crew sat at active glass desks, actually huge touch screens, each labelled with a basic function of the center. The desks clustered under a huge black dome, an electronic representation of all of space visible from the Pacific side of Terra.

A similar station, the Botswana Geostationary space hub, Bots Geo, had a dome monitoring space from the opposite side of Terra.

On the Pearl Geo dome, radiating red circles pulsed from a tiny white dot that had just popped into existence overhead. There was an interloper out there, coming down on Pearl Geo like an inter-stellar guided missile.

Seated at the security desk was a small nervous man with thinning brown hair and piercing brown eyes. He skated his fingers around on his glass desk and punched several spots on the glass. "He's not responding to our hail—not good. I'll show some authority and try a demand readout." A few more finger motions and a stream of data flowed down the glass. "Holy shit! He's from Persepolis, Proxima Centauri b, and he's just a Ford Bronco! That bucket isn't approved for interstellar, it's for junkets between here and Mars, but Proxima Centauri? No flight plan, anywhere. Looks like a joyrider. But four light-years? That would take at least a year, even in hyperspace. It just can't happen."

Security had the captain's attention. "Fall back to voice," Roper ordered. "Contact the pilot and see what's going on." The captain was a shapely attractive blonde, who wore her hair pulled back in a severe bun to maintain an image of authority.

Security did some more finger exercises and spoke into his headset mic. "Pearl Geo calling Persepolis echo three-eight-six Whiskey Sierra; report please. Over."

The control room speakers crackled with a robotic voice. "Persepolis echo three-eight-six Whiskey Sierra requests emergency priority, remote controlled docking and emergency oxygen for two. Over."

The captain was already in motion, barking orders to each of her crew. "Pilot, take control of that ship. Park it in an unused polar holding orbit while we check out its credentials." Pilot was a big Swede, with fair skin, blond hair, and blue eyes. As Pearl Geo's expert remote operator, he knew the control layout of every ship ever built on Terra or its colonies.

The captain continued, "Research, get his credentials and follow wherever they lead. Look for a trap, any kind of trap. This could be a terrorist disguised as a joy-riding kid." Research was a small African woman with a shaved head and huge circular earrings. She knew every database reachable from Pearl Geo, and she had the authority to search them all.

"Life, activate a robotic EMT and get oxygen to him in orbit. Don't risk sending a human, not until we know the risks." Life Support, usually just Life, was an Asian with the long bones of northern Japan. He was the crew's expert in operating tele-bodies, those androids that mimic a human's movements. Security, keep him talking. Find out anything you can. Did he really fly that thing her from Persepolis, and why? Is anybody alive on board? Is oxygen the only problem? Is anything lethal loose in that ship?"

While Roper was barking orders, she was also pouring coffee with the calm of a seasoned commander. This was what they were all trained to handle, a "routine emergency," and all the crew at Pearl Geo handled these unscheduled tasks with cucumber cool. Each moved easily in his Starlon shorty leotard, each displaying the six-winged logo of the United America Space Command, UASC, on the back. The midnight blue uniform was designed not to get in the way, and to show the wearer's status. Shoulders bore large gold stripes to indicate rank.

Within the hour, Pilot had the foreign ship safely in a polar orbit. Life already had a robotic tender craft waiting to synchronize with it there. The tender carried a robotic tele-body that Life control by putting on a simple exoskeleton and virtual-reality goggles. The leotard uniforms were designed with this kind of thing in mind—there was virtually nothing between the man's skin and the exoskeleton, allowing him to could control the telebody very precisely. He pressed switches on the goggles and their 3D image appeared on the room's main monitor for all to follow.

The Bronco's coupling hardware was standard. Everybody in Pearl Geo watched as Life, in his virtual reality, coupled an invisible hose to an invisible port, tightening the flange in empty air. He turned an invisible wheel and the rescue ship's compressed oxygen flooded the Bronco's life-support system. Pilot expressed it so well, "No matter how many times I see this, I never get bored. It's just so, so *bizarre*."

Life pressed some invisible buttons and the outside airlocks of the two ships became one. The tender's airgate closed and the Bronco's opened, and Life was, virtually, inside the foreign ship. "So far, so good," he reported to Captain Roper. "Nothing seems amiss, except that there's nobody here, and no breathable air. I'll do some exploring." Life moved the telebody cautiously, as though expecting danger, but he was in no danger at all. Any disaster would affect the tele-body only.

————◆◆————

Meanwhile, Research had force-pulled the ship's full identity and was searching all available databases for any information about it. "Interesting," she told her commander. "It's a private ship registered with Persepolis Space Command to a Herman Harding, a Terran who emigrated about thirty years ago, when the colony was only fifty years old. Now he collects and exports for sale in gift shops and airport lounges. You know those perfect celestine geodes that people pay ridiculous prices for? They're probably from Proxima, and probably his."

Research pressed a few more buttons on the glass. "The Bronco is a standard craft built by the new Ford assembly plant on Persepolis. Well, standard except for major extra fuel tanks and hyperspace drive. It smells of a black marketeer, but it's probably just meant to cruise around in the Proxima system for long collecting voyages without refueling. It's just possible that it can tank enough fuel to reach Terra through hyperspace, space weather permitting. There's no record of a Bronco ever doing that before, though. This is a first."

Security was having a tough time keeping the Bronco talking. The Bronco was obviously on autopilot control, and the autopilot had been told only to get the ship to Terra and to ask for emergency aid. Now it was awaiting further orders. It did not know how to chat.

Back in the Bronco, Life's telebody was exploring the ship. "Damn, this ship is crammed with oxygen tanks. There must be a hundred M60 cylinders in here. Some M250s, too. We're looking at what he cobbled together for a year of life support.

"Good Lord, here are two pressure suits sprawled on the floor, and they look occupied! Yes! There are two human beings in pressure suits connected to the ship's oxygen supply. Gimme a few minutes here. If they're still alive, I'll get them on portable air and back into the tender." Life went through the motions of disentangling the suited strangers and laying them on their backs. Then he set the controls on the forearm of each suit to give him radio voice connections to those within. He started a simple, soft chant: "Wake up, my friends. You've reached Terra, and safety. Soon you'll be in an airspace where you can shed these suits and have a nice warm bath. For now, concentrate on your breathing. Wake up, my friends…" the chant went on.

In jig time, the staff at Pearl Geo got the two men from the Bronco down to the surface and to the Emergency Room of Oahu Military Hospital, where the medical staff peeled them out of their suits. ER Orderly Rupert Jones hadn't seen anything quite like this before. "What's going on here?" he asked nobody in particular. "These guys are alive, but that's about all. They're as floppy as wet fettuccine, and God, do they stink!"

"They're in space sleep," his colleague explained. "It's kinda like hibernation. Keeps a body alive with almost no oxygen or nutrition. It's how people can endure a year or more on a spaceship without going crazy. We know how to wake them, but it'll take some time. As for the stink, well, if you'd been sealed up in the same space suit for a year, think how you'd smell. Let's get them into this bath and get them cleaned up. Pack up those suits just as they are for the investigators to smell and pick through."

An assistant scanned the wrists of both men with a handheld device, then backed away out of nose range. "They both have wrist implants," she said, "and both include full-body photo IDs. You'll be able to groom them so they'll recognize themselves when they wake up. I'm putting them both on your local monitor here."

As soon as Jones had both men floating in the big turbo-wash bath, with their heads safely braced above the water and the scrubbing jets working away, he turned his attention to the monitor. "The dark one is named John Flushing. He wears a short goatee, and he shaves his pits and pubes. We can do that for him. The redhead is Peter Harding. He wears a full beard, and only trims his body hair enough to keep it respectable. This all just screams 'Viking'! We can fix him up, too."

After two changes of water in the turbo-tub the medics pulled the strangers onto gurneys, where they dried them and trimmed nails and hair to match the photo ids. Then they trundled them upstairs where the nursing staff got them into clean beds, with oxygen cannulas and glucose/saline drips with ports for injecting the meds that would bring them around.

————•••————

The space men shared a simple hospital-green room with big windows admitting the subtropical sun, along with the heavy scent of the frangipani that bloomed profusely among the hibiscus blossoms crowding the view. The attending physician, a gorilla of a man oddly named Dr. Edwin Small, explained to his staff, "I want everything arranged to be as reassuring as possible to these men as they come to. They won't know where they are, and they need to know that they're safe. On the other hand, they mustn't think they've died and gone to heaven, either. So make everything nice, but not fancy. And whenever there's any change, call me."

The nurses agreed, and they did their best. Nurse Miriam Allison was adjusting her makeup in the room's big mirror when she heard the first intelligible sound. It sounded a little like "What the hell?" Miriam was instantly by the bedside and holding the waking man's hand. "You're safe," she said softly. "You're safe and in a hospital on Terra. Your friend is safe too." As if on cue, a matching groan came from the other bed. Miriam punched the priority call button. She would need help, and the doctor ought to be here.

Doctor Ed came at once. He made reassuring monolog as he checked vital signs and recorded things in his e-log. You boys are doing just fine. You're lucky that you got to Terra when you did, and that the fellows at Pearl Geo got you to us. You'll be tired for another week or two, so we'll be keeping you here until you've got your strength back, and some meat on those bones. That was a really long trip, and in a really small tub. You probably have quite a story to tell, but that's not for me to hear. I'll send in our Miss Brooks, our social worker, and she'll take all your information and decide what's to be done next. Now you take it easy and just rest." The men made thankful noises and then fell back to sleep, peace drawing over their faces like a window shade.

Miss Brooks waited until the men were strong enough to sit up and take simple meals. She found them on a settee, wearing plain white hospital gowns and with their arms around each other. "Call me Connie," she said, apparently embarrassed at having interrupted an intimate moment. "How are you doing? Is everything here to your liking?"

The dark man seemed to be the dominant one. "I'm John; he's Peter. We're a little concerned that we're being kept in such isolation. We feel like prisoners, not refugees. What's going on here?"

Miss Brooks came armed with the standard answers to such questions. Not needing a uniform, she had dressed to express her authority—a form-fitting white Starlon jumpsuit decorated with blue-tinged ruffles that shimmered in the traces of ultraviolet in the room lighting. "You're under a low-security quarantine. Terra has to make sure no extra-terrestrial diseases fall from the stars, as we won't have any defenses against those. It won't last long.

"They also want to keep you and the scandal press apart. You're celebrities of a sort, because strangers don't fall from space every day. The tabloids are already printing all sorts of crazy theories about who you are and why you're here. The authorities want to issue a press release countering all that, so we want to find out the truth. That's why I'm here, to start finding out the truth. "Tell me your names and where you come from. And tell me why you came all this way."

"I'm John Flushing," the dark man said. "This is my lover, Peter Harding. We came from Persepolis, because our love isn't accepted there. We want political asylum on Terra, and we want to get married." John sank back against Peter's arm, already exhausted.

Connie's eyes opened wide, but she kept her professional mien. "Take your time," she said. "We aren't in a hurry."

Peter, the one the bath attendant had called Viking, spoke up. "The colony on Persepolis is still young, and it's been through a lot of hell. Its customs come from hardship, and they're intended to ward off more hardship. It can't afford non-conforming citizens like us. There's no point in arguing with the Council. It has no mercy, only fear, fear of the unknown, fear of breaking new ground. It won't change."

It was John's turn again. "Culturally, Persepolis is about where Terra was in your dark ages. Homosexuality is forbidden, and the punishment is death. That means burning at the stake."

Connie was genuinely shocked. "How awful!" she cried. "How, how *primitive!*"

"Yes," John said. "But the colony is struggling, and I can understand it, a little bit. My father found out about us. He knows everything. He's a proud man, and he would rather turn over his only son to be burned than to have his family name disgraced. Peter's father would do the same. After we were dead they'd never speak our names again, and the colony would act as if we were never born." John coughed and sank back.

"So you came here," Connie said wonderingly. "But how did you do that? Persepolis is light-years away. It would take a starship, wouldn't it?"

Peter took it up again. "My father has an export business, and he equipped a little Ford runabout to explore the local system collecting stuff to send back here for the gift-shop trade. He really loaded it up with options, extra fuel tanks and hyperspace drive, things that are really of no use in a runabout. I guess he just wanted the hottest toy on the block. But with all that extra stuff, we thought it just might take us to Terra. So we stole the ship and all the oxygen tanks we could find, and we took the chance, even though we knew we'd probably die. We knew we'd certainly die if we stayed on Persepolis. We said our final goodbyes just before going into space sleep. That must have been about a year ago, Universal Time."

"This is like a fairy tale!" Connie exclaimed. "Why did you think you'd be better off here? Do people in the Persepolis colony know anything at all about Terra? There's almost no communication, just merchant ships, and they're pretty rare."

John reached for Peter's hand and held it warmly in both his own. "We knew that you got same-sex marriage over a century ago, before the Persepolis colony was even founded. Compared with Persepolis, Terra must be paradise, so we knew we had to come here, even if it killed us. How do we begin the asylum process? Can you help us with that?"

Connie looked like she might cry. "That's a really, *really romantic* story. Someday maybe we can write it up for people to read. Terra is probably not the paradise you've dreamed of, but I'm not the one to say. I don't know anything at all about asylum, but I'll send in one of our staff lawyers to explain your options. You might want to be careful with him. Just answer his questions and don't volunteer anything.

"Now I've tired you both out, so get some rest before your supper comes." She kissed them each on the forehead and slipped out of the room, trying to hide the unwelcome tears that she couldn't hold back any longer.

The men gained strength, and by the time the lawyer came several days later, they were dressed in street clothes provided by the hospital. Their visitor was a big swarthy man who'd seen too much sunshine and eaten too much fat. His sharkskin suit looked a bit stretched over his ample middle, and his face was covered with stubble and a worn-in grimace. "They call me Tiny," he said in a gravelly voice. "I've come to advise you on your legal status. This visit will be recorded for training purposes and quality control. Is that okay with you? Good. First I want you to tell me who you are, why you came, and what you want to do. You first." He poked a microphone in John's face.

John completely forgot Connie's warning. "I'm John Flushing," he told the mike. "and I'm here with my lover Peter. We came from the Persepolis colony, because same-sex relations are forbidden there. We want political asylum on Terra, where we understand we can live together and maybe even marry. Is that enough?"

Tiny nodded and shoved the mike into Peter's face. "I'm Peter Harding. I'm John's lover, and I want to marry him. We both know that Terra legalized same-sex marriage a very long time ago. We hope that Persepolis will eventually get there, but that won't happen in our lifetimes, so we've risked our lives to come here. We want to claim political asylum, since our lives are forfeit back home. Can you help us start that process?"

Tiny took back the mike. "Well, this is not the same Terra that legalized same-sex marriage way back then. That was at the close of the twentieth century, Universal Time. During the twenty-first century UT, there was a worldwide backlash against growing liberalism. Countries all over the world amended their constitutions to allow lifelong rulers, and pretty soon strong men took over everywhere. Right now, Terra is ruled by four autocratic dynasties, each enforcing the traditional law of his region. Here in United America, we are governed by the Diamond Dynasty, and under *The New Book of Canon Law*. Homosexuality is once again a felony here, as in all the other regions."

Both John and Peter started to speak, but Tiny stopped them with an outstretched palm. He reached into his sharkskin jacket, pulled out a large black silk scarf, draped it over his head and shoulders and put his microphone to his lips. "You and you both having confessed to the crime of homosexuality, a capital crime in the country of United America on the planet Terra, you have given up your right to a trial. I, being a licensed judge of this country, have the right and the duty to pronounce your sentence, and now I do so."

The men were dumfounded. They sat paralyzed and open-mouthed as a heavy iron portcullis slowly lowered outside their big window, crushing any hibiscus blossoms that got in the way, and polluting the smell of frangipani with machine oil.

Tiny went on. "You and you both shall be taken from this place to a United America space port, specifically, to that here on the island of Oahu. You shall be bound hand and foot. You shall be trussed into a disposable space capsule and mounted on a standard hyperspace launch vehicle. At the moment of high noon tomorrow, you shall both be shot through hyperspace directly into the surface of the sun. So says the law, and so shall it be done. May the sun burn the evil from your souls. Amen."

Tiny pulled the scarf from his head and stuffed it into his jacket as he hurried out the door. The men heard the soft click of a deadbolt. They sat for only an instant in open-mouthed astonishment. Then they both rushed the locked door with cries of anguish, clawing at its edges with naked fingernails. It was useless; the door and the wall were like one smooth surface. The window was just as impenetrable.

John and Peter fell into each other's arms in tears of despair. Their room had been built as a prison, and Tiny had sealed their only escape.

And their doom.

Mama Was a Marple

Mama was the youngest of a huge brood of English siblings. Aunt Jane was the eldest, and a good twenty-five years older than mama. Grandma must have delivered a new bundle of joy to Grandpa Marple just about every year, and she must have changed life later than most women. You could say that her profession was being pregnant. How she lived to the ripe old age of ninety-two without dying of exhaustion is a mystery to me. Maybe she had better vegetables than we do, as Truman Capote once said.

Most of my aunts and uncles inherited Grandma's robust health, and most of them produced several offspring, though not as rampantly as their mother. I have more cousins than I can keep track of. I used to keep a notebook of them, but after line fifty-nine I just stopped.

Of course, all those cousins are also Aunt Jane's nieces and nephews. They're all over England, all over the commonwealth, and all over the Continent. So far as I know, we're the only branch of the family in America. That's fine by me; I like to stay out of sight and out of mind. We all adore Aunt Jane, because, as you probably know, she's sort of world famous. She keeps solving murders that baffle the local police, wherever she goes. It seems that murder follows the woman around—I sometimes wonder why the authorities don't investigate *her*. But luckily, she doesn't often travel too far from St. Mary Mead. There have been exceptions of course, notably that trip to the Caribbean, where she not only solved a murder, but prevented another.

Like everybody else, I do adore Aunt Jane, but at the same time, I don't exploit my relation to her. Some of the cousins do, especially the ones in law enforcement. Timmy Barton, who's a detective in Plymouth, a long way from St. Mary Mead, asks her advice by phone on every crime he investigates. Then he takes credit for solving the case, and nobody ever knows it was actually Aunt Jane who did it. And she lets him get away with it. Go figure.

For me, though, being related to Aunt Jane is a liability. It's like being Lucy Arnaz and working for a director who expects Lucille Ball. I hear that Lucy is gutsy, and able to handle herself when that happens, but I'm not that self-confident. In fact, I've gone from job to job, looking for permanent anonymity, and never, so far, finding it.

It ought to be easy. Mama married an American named Tommy Baker and settled down in Atlanta. There'd be no reason anybody would suspect her of notorious connections, and she was as determined to keep it quiet as I was. She doesn't like the idea of being invited to every boring ladies' group in town just so they can stare at her as if she's a two-headed cat.

When I was about fourteen, I checked out my Dad's family history back a couple of generations, and I didn't find anything alarming. We were no kin to Ma Baker and the Baker Boys, nor to Josephine Baker, nor to Norma Jeane Baker, aka Marilyn Monroe, nor to anybody else anybody has ever heard of. We were safely ordinary on Dad's side.

But not on Mom's, of course. I would tell people who asked after her, "Oh, she came over from England, by herself, and we aren't in touch with whatever family she had there." That was true, or pretty nearly true. I implied that we didn't know her family, but in fact, I had that book of cousins, and I did always send Aunt Jane a card on her birthday.

That kind of dissembling got me through college and into my first job as a bookkeeper at Applebaum Business Associates in Peachtree Center. I was just fine for two whole years, nobody suspected who my aunt was and so nobody expected me to be like her. And then, in a problem-solving session in the board room, my boss blurted out, "Come on, man, surely you inherited at least some of your family's problem-solving talents!" I just stared at him as my world turned upside down. Probably looking like a zombie with adenoids, I just stood up and walked out of the room, out of the building, and out of the job.

It was two days before I found my way home, and two months before I found another job. One of the art galleries on Bennett Street in Buckhead needed a bookkeeper. I applied and I got the job. My boss, Zelda Kenworth, was an atrocious woman of forty who dressed to shock. One day she came in wearing a red Rudi Gernreich monokini. I don't know where she got it, because Rudi only made them in black. But she got tired of it before lunch, and changed into a clear vinyl chemise worn over several strategically glued on black patches. It must have been hot as hell under there.

Anyway, I humored Zelda for over a year. I set up her parties, engraved her invites, stocked her bar and tended it, and pretty much did everything she needed done, because she did pretty much nothing except pose and drink gin. Eventually, she expected me to be her bouncer, and to bodily throw out anybody who displeased her in any trivial way. That was enough. I told her to do her own dirty work. She grabbed my tie and held me at a stiff arm's length. "That old aunt of yours has been praised for her fluffy ruthlessness, and that's what I expect of you. You will be my male eye candy until I need muscle, and then you will swell up and turn green and vicious like that Hulk fellow. Be that or be out." I dropped three of her priceless champagne flutes onto her marble-tiled floor and marched out. I never got my final paycheck, but I felt plenty compensated in about a month when the morning paper showed a picture of her being arrested for money laundering and pushing fake art. Fortunately, she was the vindictive sort, and she must have burned all the records of my employment.

My next job was with Lockheed Martin up in Marietta. I put money down on a condo on Alday Lane and got a mortgage that I could not possibly afford. But having one of those human breasts in which hope springs eternal, I set up housekeeping anyway. My Lockheed pay was good, and I figured if I avoided people like Zelda for a couple of years, I could eventually come out ahead. I was wrong.

Two weeks into my new job, just when I was beginning to feel like I belonged, my boss explained, "We're a defense contractor, as you know, so you probably know we checked you out pretty thoroughly before we made you that offer. We like your old auntie, the one called *Nemesis* and we hope you have some of her balls. Next Monday we're opening negotiations on a really critical job, and we need a really tough negotiator. We think you're it." I took a cab to my realtor's office and put the condo back on the market.

And that's how it's been. Aunt Jane looms large over the entire world, and there's no place to hide. When you're related to one of the most formidable criminologists in England, you aren't allowed to be ordinary. I stumbled from job to hopeless job for about twenty years. Eventually, though, Dad died and left me a nice portfolio. I just stopped trying to work and lived on my interest and Bourbon.

And then Alfred came. Alfred is one of my cousins, but on the Baker side. He's apparently a very well-heeled cousin, because he doesn't work and he lives in a condo in

Aspen. I met him at a mid-winter Baker family reunion in Palm Springs, and we hit it off right away. After a couple of nights together in Palm Springs we both thought maybe this would grow into an actual relationship. Alfred invited me to spend some time on the slopes, in a trial partnership, and of course, I welcomed the idea. I'm only a mediocre schusser, and when I'm on skis, there's only one thing on my mind, and that's staying alive. It's the best way to rid my mind of whatever demons are torturing me on any given day. And for a couple of days it worked just great. Alfred knew about Aunt Jane, but he understood my reluctance to talk, so he never brought her up in conversation. I was safe at last.

Then some evildoer, probably somebody Aunt Jane had fingered, moved a pine tree into my path on the advanced slope, and I wound up in an infirmary for a day or so. When I got back to Alfred's condo, he was a regular Florence Nightingale. "Would you like anything with your Bourbon?" he asked.

"I think there's some OxyContin in my bag over there. That would be nice." I was thinking about passing out in an alcoholic and opiate haze.

Alfred observed me quizzically. "I'm surprised. I thought you'd probably be taking the advice of your great-great-great Aunt Mary, and toughing it out."

"I don't have a great-great-however many greats Aunt Mary." I said. "And even if I did, I wouldn't be looking for her advice. Will you bring me the pills, or do I have to crawl over there like a sea slug?"

"Take it easy, man. I'll get your stuff. But yes, you do have a multi-great Aunt Mary. You probably know her by her married name, Eddy."

My mind froze. Mary Eddy? *Mary Baker Eddy?* **Oh My God!**

Another Way It Coulda 'Appened

Keep that title in mind—it "coulda 'appened"—because none of these characters is derived from, or is meant to bear any resemblance to, Marcel Duchamp, Pablo Picasso, or any of their mistresses.

I met Piggy in 1901. I 'member 'cause it was one-a them bloody memorial parties for Victoria. This one was at th' Rose and Madder in Soho, so it was fulla starvin' artists and bloody Tin Pan Alley music. 'Course I weren't no starvin' artist, but I was a starvin' barmaid, so I fit in very well.

Anyhow, Piggy was dancin' starkers on a table. Several blokes were. After all, Victoria was dead, Th' Playboy Prince was ascendin', and it was a' excuse ta party, weren't it? Somebody there gave a sorta eulogy: "For 'er first two decades she was a pampered lass; then for two more decades she was always in a family way; finally for four decades she was in everlastin' mournin', and so were we. Now at last, *she's gone*, and *we're free!*" 'Course that was all bloody rubbish, weren't it? Nobody in Soho paid no attention ta what went on in Buck 'Ouse, or who was doin' it, so Edward wouldn't make no difference, would 'e? So it weren't like breakin' a bloody Champagne bottle, but it was a' excuse ta drink. Not that any-a us *needed* a' excuse ta drink, mind you.

Th' party went til all 'ours, and then I wound up goin' 'ome wiv Piggy to 'is penny-dreadful starvin'-artist's garret. We 'it it orf all right, and inside-a a month I moved in. I lived there for eleven bloomin' years, and in all that time, I never learned Piggy's real name! When you're a starvin' artist in

Edwardian Soho, you prob'ly don't need one. 'E didn't use me name, either. 'E called me "Mimi," 'cause th' bloody garret reminded 'ima *La Bohème*. It was that dreadful.

I never did understand Piggy's art stuff. Ta me it looked like kiddies' bloody chalk scratchin's on slateboards. But since it was oil on canvas it was s'posed ta be respectable, and a man who made 'is livin' paintin' it was s'posed ta be respectable too.

Trouble was, Piggy didn't actsh'ly make a bloody livin' paintin'. 'E took 'is stuff out ta show people who ran shops, but nobody ever bought nothin', or even offered ta let 'im 'ang 'is stuff. So our garret walls were covered wiv bloody pictures nobody wanted. What money Piggy did make was by drawin' caricaturesa strollers in 'Yde Park or Regent's Park and chargin' a tanner. Almost anybody would give 'im bloody sixpence for a funny cartoon they could take 'ome and show orf ta mates who came ta tea.

What we actsh'ly lived on was wat I made daytimes as a clark at Blair's greengrocers, and nighttimes slingin' pints at th' bloody Rose and Madder. It weren't much, but I got ta eat at th' pub, and I got ta take 'ome somea th' bloody produce that got too rotten ta sell, and that 'elped us live cheap.

I musta loved Piggy a lot, at least ta start wiv, ta put up wiv all that. But love ain't always forever, and a lot 'appened ta stretch ours ta th' breakin'. Our lives were bloody mis'rable. Jus' like Mimi, we never 'ad no money. And finally, I lost Piggy's baby. A course I told meself it was for th' best. We couldn't afford a baby. I'da been a bloody awful mother. And when I thinka Piggy as a father, well…

———◆◆◆———

Th' starta th' end for me and Piggy was th' first paintin'a wat I call *Th' Series*. Piggy came back from th' Park bringin' a pencil sketcha two young ladies. "Julie and Clair waited," 'is nibs said, "'til I'd sketched 'em before rememberin' neivera 'em 'ad brought a bloody purse. Silly trollops!" But it was a bloomin' good sketch, and Piggy sat and stared at it for a long time. Then 'e went over ta 'is easel and commenced ta copy it in oils. Finally 'e called me over ta 'ave a butcher's hook. "'Ere they are," 'e said. "Whaddaya think?"

"They're bloody ghastly," I says. "In your sketch they were pretty, laughin' girls, but 'ere they're bloody witches screamin' at th' sky. Wots that all abaat?"

"That's art, you crumpet, modern art, not that bloody Renaissance stuff. 'Appiness is th' enemy-a art." Piggy wrote *Julie Penderling and Clair Chase* on th' backa th' picture, and 'e took it around ta th' shops, but, like always, nobody bit. So it got 'ung on th' wall just like all th' other failures, but th' firsta th' bloody *Series*.

———•••———

Piggy used ta 'ave long, deep depressions. 'E'd sit in that bloody garret and stare at th' walls, or out th' one norf-facin' dormer winder, for 'ours. Piggy said a painter 'ad ta 'ave a norf-facin' winder, and that it didn't really matter wat it looked out on, long as it looked norf. Ours looked out on a steep roof wiv bloody chimneypots that poured out dirty stinkin' smoke, even in th' summertime, since people still 'ad ta cook, didn't they? We didn't even try ta open that bloody winder 'cept in August, when th' bloody 'eat was worse than th' bloody soot. It got gruesome 'ot in th' garret, so we usually went about starkers in th' summertime. It didn't matter; nobody ever came ta call. And even if somebody did, it would just be onea Piggy's bloody starvin' artist mates, so it still didn't matter. Victoria was dead, 'member, and these were Edward's times.

Once, in onea 'is blue funks, Piggy brought a stool and sat in fronta th' greengrocers shop. 'E sat there mosta th' day, just starin' at th' wooden crates set up outside ta show orf th' bloody fruits and vegetables in their various rotten states. I just pretended I didn't know 'im, buta course Mr. Blair knew I did. Piggy didn't bother th' bloody customers, so Mr. Blair didn't bother 'im, and in th' middlea th' afternoon, Piggy picked up 'is stool and left.

When I got 'ome, there was a new picture on th' easel. It was a bloody smudgea gray and blue, but if I tried I could make out a wooden crate filled wiv fruit. There was one bloody light bulb 'angin' over it all, bright blue, but not lightin' up nothin'. And everything was dun in little dots—no brush strokes. "Pointillism," Piggy explained. "It's different."

Still Life wiv Angst? I suggested. I liked ta name Piggy's stuff.

"No Mimi, I call it *Moody Renderin' a Pear Case*. Me muse likes th' ringa it. It's me." Well, I couldn't argue wiv that. It bloody *was* Piggy. But then, so was *Still Life wiv Angst*. Like always, nobody wanted *Pear Case*, so it got 'ung on th' bloody wall as th' seconda *Th' Series*.

---•••---

I 'onestly don't know wat brought on th' next paintin'a *Th' Series*. I came 'ome from th' greengrocers and found this *thing* on th' easel. There was this big bloody petrol tractor crashin' right through wat looked like a 'orse paddock, and tearin' it ta bits. There were several things that looked like screamin' 'orses and bulls, some lookin' chopped into bloody pieces. It was all red and black, and it was th' most 'orrible thing Piggy 'ad ever dun. I shuddered and said, *Rest in Pieces*? *Th' 'Orse and Carnage*?

But Piggy already 'ad 'is bloody mind made up. *Rude Upendin'a Mare Place*, 'e declared. "Futurism. It's Italian." After starin' stupidly at *Mare Place* for a couplea 'ours, Piggy took it and 'ung it beside *Pear Case*. 'E didn't even take it out ta th' shops. 'E knew it was that bloody bad.

———•••———

Then one day Piggy came 'ome all in a bloody lather. 'E'd been ta some lecture on stroboscopic photography and th' cinema, and 'e was all a-bubblin' over wiv new ideas. 'E made about a 'undred pencil sketches, throwin' wadsa paper all over th' bloody floor, and 'e finally marched ta 'is easel and started paintin' like a mad man. When 'e was through, wat 'e 'ad was different from anythin' else 'e'd ever dun. Well, except for th' stuff in th' background. That was just like th' resta *Th' Series*.

"Bloody 'ell!" I said, "That bloomin' fist is comin' right outa that picture and at me! Wanna call it *Leadin' Wiv Your Left*?"

"No Mimi," 'e says. "It's *Dude Defendin' a Fair Face*!" And it was true; in one cornera th' bloody background was th' fair face, a kneelin' creature kinda like *Clair Chase*, starin' up wiv this shell-shocked look. Th' main image was a bloody fist, or more like a buncha fists, curvin' outa th' canvas and getting' bigger and bolder 'til one final fist busted out at ya and made ya wanna bloody duck. In a top corner was th' Dude's face, attached ta all th' fists and wearin' a bloody top 'at like Alice's mad 'atter. Th' fists were dun like nothin' I'd ever seen before. "Cubism," Piggy said. "It's new."

I didn't believe it, but *Fair Face* actsh'ly interested at least onea th' local shops. It 'ung there for about six months before Piggy gave up and brought it back ta 'ang in th' bloody garret wiv th' resta *Th' Series*. After *Fair Face* came 'ome, Piggy was downcast for a long time. 'E did 'ave moments when 'e got bloody excited wiv th' possibilitiesa 'is new cubist and kinetic ideas. But 'e didn't produce nothin' new for a long spell.

———•••———

Then it 'appened! It was an unbearable 'ot day—a real scorcher—in August, and we'd opened th' bloody dormer winder ta try ta get any air that might be stirrin'. We were covered wiv sweat and th' bloody grime from a dozen neighbors' cookstoves. I was tryin' ta get a nap between Blair's and th' pub. Our bloody garret roof was just as steep as th' one out th' winder, and even though there wasn't much floor space, there was plenty-a bloody 'eight. There was room up above for a little sleepin' loft, but it was bloody 'otter up there, so finally I gave up and started down th' bloomin' ladder.

Piggy looked up and did a bloody double take. 'E looked electrocuted. "Stop!" 'e yelled. "Go back up! Come back down!" I did, and ag'in, and maybe five times, while 'e just barked bloody orders and stared. Then 'e dashed ta 'is easel chatterin' like a bloody madman, and I pulled on a frock and went out ta earn our livin' at th' bloody pub.

I was dead tired when I got back, and Piggy was passed out, so I didn't look at th' bloody easel 'til th' next mornin'. When I woke up, Piggy was up and dressed and pantin' like a puppy about ta get a bone. "Whaddaya think?"

Well, I didn't know wat ta think, did I? Th' paintin' was a lot like *Fair Face*, wiv a lota duplicate bloody images and clear notionsa movin', but wiv nonea th' crazy stuff from *Th' Series*. But wat was it that was movin'? Bunchesa bloody rectangles. Nothin' I could figure out wat was. *Explosion in a Shingle Factory*? I suggested.

"No, you crumpet, that's *you!*" Piggy said. "That's you comin' down those bloody stairs yesterday, and it's th' best thing I've ever dun!" 'E grabbed th' canvas and ran out th' bloomin' door, and I never saw 'im again!

I guess Piggy musta sold *Explosion*, 'cause a couplea weeks later I got a bloomin' bank cheque for £300 in th' post, wi' no way to tell who from. That was more money than I'd ever 'ad at one time in me life, and I spent it well. I quit th' greengrocers job and got some bloody sleep. I invested a few bob in th' strugglin' Rose and Madder, not even guessin' that years later I'd come ta own it outright. I moved outa Piggy's bloody garret inta a real flat wiv two winders and some air. I left all Piggy's stuff in case 'e came back, or for th' landlord ta deal wiv if 'e didn't. But for some reason, I took *Th' Series* wiv me. Not that I fancied th' bloody pictures, but somehow it seemed like I oughta keep somethin' from them eleven bloody yearsa me life, and there weren't nothin' else.

--------•••--------

I musta 'ad a soft spot for starvin' artists, 'cause I ran though a bloody lota 'em in th' next few years. I told people I ran a' artist laundry, 'cause I picked 'em up, cleaned 'em up, and taught 'em 'ow ta stand on their own two feet. When they could, they did, and I bloody sent 'em packin'. Somea 'em 'id all right. Some even paid their bloody rent.

About twenty-five years after Piggy done a runner, I finally took over th' bloody Rose and Madder, and I was a respectable businesswoman. I redecorated th' place. I threw out all th' bloody *art nouveau* junk and got some bloody art deco junk instead. I renamed th' bloody place th' Scott and Zelda, in 'opesa attrac'in' a better crowd, a' idea that never really worked out too well.

It was about then I took up wiv this Mikel fella, a Basque painter who 'ad a' bloody education and a fam'ly name, and actsh'ly sold stuff. I moved into 'is much-better flat, and I brought *Th' Series* wiv me. Th' flat was bloody 'uge, wiv 'igh ceilings and this big separate studio where Mikel could work in th' glowa 'is obligatory norf-facin' winders. Mikel was fascinated wiv *Th' Series*. 'E 'ung all th' bloody paintin's on this one walla th' studio, and 'e'd study 'em for 'ours and 'ours. "Well, whaddaya thinka 'im?" I finally inquired.

"I think he was mad," Mikel replied. "But maybe mad like Van Gogh. Did he ever do crazy stuff? Did he ever, say, cut off his ear?"

"No," I said, thinkin' back. "I'da remembered that. 'E was fonda runnin' about starkers and guzzlin' cheap wine. Nobody thought that was crazy, not then and there, but everything in 'is paintin's looks crazy. Whaddaya think that Dr. Freud fella would say about 'em?"

"I think Dr. Freud's crazy enough for both of them," Mikel replied. "But he'd probably say something about personality dissociation. Looks like Piggy just staggered from one thing to another, and never did decide just wat he was or wat he wanted to be. His cubist stuff showed real promise, and he should have done more of that. Anyway, he's probably into Dada by now." I didn't ask wat that meant. Some things a decent girl don't want ta know.

———•••———

Th' studio was Mikel's private workshop. I stayed out unless I was invited, and that usually 'appened when 'e'd finished somethin' and 'e called me in ta make admirin' noises. Once, after several crazy weeksa workin' nonstop, 'e called me in ta admire 'is bloody *magnum opus*. 'E said that meant 'is greatest work. Well, bloody magnum it was! It completely covered th' twenty-five-foot south walla th' studio, and it was so awful I wanted ta go right back out agin.

It was inspired by *Th' Series*. I could see that. There was *Julie Penderlin'* and *Clair Chase*, screamin' at th' sky, only now one was 'oldin' a dead baby. There was th' bare light bulb from *Pear Case*, 'angin' like a' bloody evil eye over th' 'ole thing. There was this butchered 'orse and bull from *Mare Place*, and th' shell-shocked face from *Fair Face*. And there was other crazy stuff. I shuddered and I stared, and I stared and I shuddered. "*Gruesome, Rendin' Nightmare Place!*" I gasped, rememberin' th' namesa th' paintin'sa *Th' Series*.

"No," Mikel said. "This is about a real horror that happened in a real place back home in Spain. This has to be shown where people will see it and remember. And it has to be named *Guernica*. That's the town where it happened."

And it *was* shown. After Mikel figured out 'ow ta get it outa th' bloody flat, it 'ung at th' 1937 Paris International Exposition for that 'ole bloody fair. Since then it, or copiesa it, 'ang in important places all 'round th' bloody world, so people do remember. And Mikel's work is famous.

Or is it Piggy's work? I never did find out wot 'appened ta Piggy. But somethin' 'appened one time when I was waddin' up mackerel bones in old newspaper for th' bloody dustbin. Somethin' in a' old *London Times* caught me eye. There'd been a' exhibitiona Cubist stuff, and onea 'em was called *Nude Descendin' a Staircase*. It sounded like what Piggy woulda called me *Explosion in a Shingle Factory*. Maybe he'd been workin' up ta that name all th' bloody time. There was *Julie Penderlin' and Clair Chase*, *Moody Renderin'a Pear Case*, *'Rude Upendin' a Mare Place*, and *Dude Defendin' a Fair Face*. *Nude Descendin' a Staircase* would be th' next one, wouldn't it? I didn't recognize th' artist's name, but then, like I said, I never did learn Piggy's real name, or even if 'e 'ad one.

Well, I wish 'im well, wherever 'e is.

Whoever 'e is.

Whatever 'e is.

Chronos

He sat there on the curb of the beach parking lot, lost in his own world. He wore long pants and long sleeves, and a neck scarf, a stark contrast to the bikini-clad throngs that washed around him like the waves on the nearby strand. Sunken eyes, hiding between a tweed tam and bushy moustache and beard, peered out into space as though there were nothing there.

He held a twelve-string guitar, which he stroked tenderly, expertly, casually, lovingly, as though he and the instrument were one flesh, as though fingers and strings had never been apart. He sang softly, almost to himself, as though the song were his reason for being, and yet the keen timbre of his voice pierced the murmur of the crowd and carried far in all directions.

He must have known a million ballads, and he sang through them all, one by one, never seeming to repeat. Except for one song, a sort of theme song, a song that he sang between almost every ballad, a song that the beach regulars came to know by heart.

> *I am the guy who takes time from the future*
> *And makes it turn into the past.*
> *If it weren't for me, all the misery you see*
> *Would last and last and last.*
>
> *No need to ask what I'm doing today;*
> *I'm sittin' here whilin' the hours away.*

It's tough work, but someone must do it, they say,
Or there'll be the Devil to pay.
There'll be the Devil to pay.

You'd think that a work as important as this
Would have a big government grant.
But it just isn't so; as endowments go,
Washington won't, or can't.

But you can fix that; drop a coin in the hat
Whenever it passes your way.
Or better, a bill; put it there in the till,
And keep time just rolling away.
No need to ask…

Ginger-haired UCLA student Sally Armstrong was one of those regulars, and she knew the song by heart. She even hummed it while she did her chores at the big university library, carefully reshelving books pulled from the stacks by other students in their research. She was even humming it when she picked up her twin sister Halley at LAX.

"Oh, look at you!" Halley cried. "I'd forgotten just how gorgeous you are!"

Sally giggled. "Kidder! You know I look exactly like you! You're just talking about yourself!"

Halley wrinkled her nose and touched it to her sister's. "Now you'd better learn to take a compliment wherever it comes from. Someday we'll both be old hags, and you'll wish somebody would notice. Anybody. And you did wear the tartan, just as we agreed!"

"Of course," Sally rejoined. "When we bought them at Bloomingdale's, we said we'd probably never have a chance to wear them together. Well, here we are!" The girls wore identical blue and green clan Armstrong tartan outfits, and with their short red hair, they could have been mistaken for kilted Highlanders.

They laughed and hugged and hugged and laughed and acted like silly girls, talking all at once. "Tell me about New York!" "Tell me about college!" "You got a job?" "You got a man?" "How long can you stay?" "I'm starving!" "Let's get out of here!" "Let's get my bag!" "What will you want to do?" "I want to see everything in L.A., *everything!*"

So Sally spent two weeks, and a lot of credit card, showing Halley all the tourist stuff in and around L.A. Hollywood, what was left of it; Sunset Strip; Muscle Beach; the Hollywood Bowl; a Symphony at the Disney; a rock concert at Staples Center; a game at Dodger Stadium; the Griffith Park Planetarium; endless museums; night clubs; Rodeo Drive; shopping; more identical outfits; the works. Halley was just inexhaustible.

Sally was not. Sally was tired. "Today," she proclaimed, "we're gonna just lie on the beach and rest. We'll pick up a picnic lunch at Kosherama on the way. I've got two sets of earbuds, so we can share some of the old songs from when we were kids. That's bound to bring back lots of memories to talk about."

———•••———

And that's how Halley met Chronos. More accurately, that's how Halley first saw the weird fellow who sang about time. He was certainly one of the sights to see, and Sally found a parking place near the soft guitar music.

"They call him Chronos," she said, walking on after dropping a dollar into his open guitar case. I don't know if that's really his name. Maybe they just call him that because he sings about time. He's always here, or somewhere around here, daytimes. At sunset he packs up his guitar and his earnings and walks away down the beach. Nobody knows where he goes. They say that people who have tried to follow him always lose him somehow. That sounds kinda crazy, though."

"Not crazy at all," Halley responded. "He can't afford for anybody to see him get into his big Bentley and head for his obscene Bel Air mansion. For him, losing a tail is a survival skill."

Sally regarded her reproachfully. "Oh ye of little faith. Don't you ever just have fun with something?"

Halley decided to change the subject. "Why do you have to refile all those books, anyhow? Why can't the people who pull them out just put them back?"

"Oh, you know why that is," her twin explained. "What if somebody put one back in the wrong place? In a library, a misfiled book is a lost book. Over the years, we'd lose track of everything." She laughed mischievously. "Besides, I need the job."

------•◦•------

Sally and Halley lived it up for two weeks, and then it was time for Halley to go back to New York. As Sally drove her to LAX in her yellow VW bug, they sang the song that was stuck in both their heads, "I am the guy who takes time from the future..."

"I think I should curse you for letting me hear that song," Halley said. "Now I'm stuck with it forever." She suddenly brightened. "But there's one good thing; now I'm finally rid of 'It's a Small, Small World'!"

Then she sobered again. "Do you think there's anything to his notion of moving time from the future to the past? I mean it really does flow that way, you know. Not that anybody needs to help it, do they?"

"Well, do you remember when we watched that movie *The Langoliers*? There were these great big Pacman-like monsters that ate up all the world in the immediate past. Then they skipped around the present and used their chompings to build the world back up in the immediate future, just in time for the present to find it. Of course, nobody in the present could see them, because they weren't there in the present. It's not exactly the same, but it's the same kind of notion. They're both crazy, but they're both fun to think about. And now we have to get you in there before you miss your plane!"

———◆◆◆———

Sally saw her sister through security and watched her disappear into the throat of the jetway. "The future is swallowing you up," she thought sadly. "When will I see you again?"

She got her little VW bug and drove out Century Boulevard. As she merged onto the 405, she realized that she was humming *the song* again. She flipped on the radio and pushed the button for the Oldies station, hoping to fill her mind with something else.

"And that was Les Paul and Mary Ford with *Tiger Rag*," the announcer said. "What a master guitar player that man was! His work on electric guitars and multi-track recording changed popular music forever!

"And speaking of guitars, we just got a bulletin from the CHP. Apparently there's been a big traffic pileup up on Will Rogers Beach. A high-speed chase down PCH crashed into a parking lot, with parked cars destroyed and several casualties. Apparently one of the victims was the sidewalk musician they call Chronos, and..."

But Sally didn't hear the rest of the report. Traffic was slowing down fast, and she needed to pay attention to driving. She flipped her blinker for a lane change, and the blinker clicked slowly, then slower yet, then so very slowly… everything was stopping. Sally started to panic. She screamed, and the pitch of her scream dropped like a slide whistle, down to the deep bass of a bottom organ pipe. She slipped into a catatonic state.

And all over the world, the Devil took his pay.

Acknowledgments

I am indebted to many people for their help, in shaping not just this little book, but my life. I'm not saying that these people would approve of everything in this book, only that they have helped me.

First, the two ladies in the dedication. Leona Carscallen Berglund was my high-school English teacher. She saw promise in me, and despite the awful boor that I must have been at seventeen, she played Mame to my Patrick and showed me that the universe is a far larger place than I had ever imagined. It is because of Leona's patronage that I have dared to live my life.

Elizabeth Stephenson, a renaissance woman and a shining star in Sky Valley, California, took pleasure in my little stories, encouraged me, and introduced me to people who gave me invaluable criticism and encouragement. It is because of Elizabeth that I got off my butt and published.

Two writing seminars have helped me. Author David Wallace has held creative writing seminars at the Palm Springs LGBT Center and later at the Mizell Senior Center of Palm Springs. He and the participants in his seminars have criticized me roundly, but always kindly and usefully. I'm especially grateful that David consented to write the foreword to this volume.

Author, director, actor, and playwright Andy Harmon is the facilitator of the Writers Studio at the CVRep (Coachella Valley Repertory Theater) Conservatory. He and his group have also given me valuable constructive criticism. Because of the different viewpoint of this group, their input has extended and complemented that of the Wallace group. I owe them both.

I'm indebted to London-born Anita Harmon for her advice on things Cockney in the tale "Another Way It Could o' Appened."

Finally, Tim Summerlee has read and critiqued various drafts, and he has given me invaluable advice.

About the Author

Harry Neil is not your ordinary California Desert Eccentric. He describes himself as a DRIT, a "desert rat in training," and he eschews the superfluous things around him: Twitter, clothing, hip-hop, the right side of his full beard, etc.

Harry is a retired computer programmer, and he is, he says, "probably the only man to have had a wet dream about a computer program."

Harry gets much of his material from his birthplace in North Carolina's Cape Fear Basin; however, he is a permanent desert transplant, preferring sidewinders to water moccasins and cactus to kudzu.

Harry is especially happy writing melodrama or farce, but he is comfortable with other genres as well. This collections of "short pieces"—only some of which can be called "stories"—range far and wide, and have something for everyone.

CPSIA information can be obtained
at www.ICGtesting.com
Printed in the USA
FSHW021209100921
84630FS

9 781734 260120